Deep Water

Deep Water

JAMIE SUMNER

ATHENEUM BOOKS FOR YOUNG READERS
New York London Toronto Sydney New Delhi

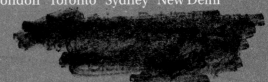

ATHENEUM BOOKS FOR YOUNG READERS

An imprint of Simon & Schuster Children's Publishing Division

1230 Avenue of the Americas, New York, New York 10020

This book is a work of fiction. Any references to historical events, real people, or real places are used fictitiously. Other names, characters, places, and events are products of the author's imagination, and any resemblance to actual events or places or persons, living or dead, is entirely coincidental.

Simon & Schuster: Celebrating 100 Years of Publishing in 2024

For information about special discounts for bulk purchases, please contact Simon & Schuster Special Sales at 1-866-506-1949 or business@simonandschuster.com.

The Simon & Schuster Speakers Bureau can bring authors to your live event. For more information or to book an event, contact the Simon & Schuster Speakers Bureau at 1-866-248-3049 or visit our website at www.simonspeakers.com.

Interior design by Karyn Lee

The text for this book was set in Utopia Std.

Manufactured in the United States of America

0324 BVG

First Edition

10 9 8 7 6 5 4 3 2 1

Library of Congress Cataloging-in-Publication Data

Names: Sumner, Jamie, author.

Title: Deep water / Jamie Sumner.

Description: First edition. | New York : Atheneum Books for Young Readers, 2024. | Audience: Ages 10 and Up. | Summary: Twelve-year-old Tully's attempt to swim across Lake Tahoe after a heartbreaking loss and become the youngest person to complete the famous "Godfather" swim takes a dangerous turn, forcing her to choose between safety and a win that could change everything.

Identifiers: LCCN 2023005417 | ISBN 9781665935067 (hardcover) | ISBN 9781665935081 (ebook)

Subjects: CYAC: Novels in verse. | Long distance swimming—Fiction. | Loss—Fiction. | Mothers—Fiction. | Best friends—Fiction. | Friendship—Fiction. | LCGFT: Novels in verse.

Classification: LCC PZ7.5.S86 De 2024 | DDC [Fic]—dc23

LC record available at https://lccn.loc.gov/2023005417

For Jody

PROLOGUE

My Mother Told Me

The problem with letting someone else tell your story
is that they always get it wrong.

They'll shove their morals
and personality
and biases
and blind spots
and irritations
into it.

Which means the one thing you can never do
is let another person speak for you.

That's what she said
one day before she left.

I'll never know her story
because she never gave me time
to ask.

Now that she's gone,

while I'm out here
on the not-so-still waters,
almost all alone,
there's no one to tell my story to.

Because nobody listens to a kid.
Instead, they tell you what you did
    or didn't do.
What you are
    and are not about.

The thing about being twelve
is that all anybody thinks to do
is talk *at* you.

At least out here,
the water drowns her silence
and the rest of the world's noise.

HOUR ONE

How It Starts

Air temp: 44 degrees.
Water temp: 68 degrees.
Body temp: 98.3 degrees.
Mental state of swimmer: Calm. Loose. Ready.
Mental state of support crew: Unknown and highly variable.

Arch looks like he's going to puke—
hands on knees,
head down like a dog,
orange life vest bunched around his ears.

Poor Arch.
He wasn't meant for the open water.

He's a worrier.
You can't be a worrier and a swimmer.
The water demands trust.
Whatever conditions . . .
Whatever's below . . .
Whatever your head tells you . . .
You have to believe you're going to make it
to the other side.

The minute you start to doubt yourself,
you make mistakes.
The water doesn't forgive mistakes.

Me?
I'm a believer
in the power of the water
and in myself.
I don't make mistakes.

While we're still on shore,
Arch adjusts his life vest and breathes in through his nose.
I check his watch.

"5:58 a.m. You've got two minutes to get it together," I say,
and look out over the dark blue of Lake Tahoe,
which is just beginning to twitch awake.

"Tully, I can't," Arch says, like he has a choice.

"You have to.
You swore it."

I don't remind him when or why he swore it.

He picks up the kayak,
drags it to the water's edge.
He remembers.

Behind me, Cave Rock would cast a shadow
if the sun were high enough.
They call her Lady of the Lake.
If you squint hard enough,
the rock looks like a woman.

I think it's a stretch.
If you try hard enough,
anything can look like anything.
Unless it disappears,
and then all the imagining in the world
won't turn it into what you want,
which brings me back to today.

"One minute," Arch whispers,
and swipes his dark hair out of his eyes.

We look out over the water.
I nudge his shoulder.
"You can do it."

He nudges me back.
"That's what I'm supposed to say to you."
This will be the last time we touch for at least six hours—
if I do this right,
which I will,
because I do not make mistakes.

I pull my goggles down and step in.
Lady of the Lake, wish me luck.
Not that I believe in luck.
Or second chances.
But I believe in the power of the water
to do what it needs to do
for me,
for Mom.

"Call it," I say to Arch,
who swallows,
lifts up his phone,
presses record.

"Time is 6:00 a.m.
Participant has left the natural shore."
His voice breaks on *shore*,
but he keeps going:

"The marathon swim has begun."

68 Degrees

The second I go under,
goose bumps march like tiny ants
up   down
      and
my arms and legs.

Tight legs don't want to bend.
Tight shoulders don't want to stretch.
Tight lungs feel the squeeze of cold water
and squeeze back.

This is how it always is
in the beginning
before the body makes friends with the elements.

68 degrees might not sound too bad
if you're lying on a beach somewhere
under a shining sun
on top of warm sand.

But 68 degrees
under a gray sky
in deep water
with nothing
but your swimsuit
and body fat

to protect you
is no day at the beach.

"Safety check!"
Arch yells on my right.

I can feel him there,
slicing through the calm lake
in his blue kayak
and orange life vest,
hyperventilating only a little.

"It's been two minutes, Arch.
Give me a second to adjust,"
I say around the clacking of teeth in my skull.

I force my arms to reeeeeeach forward
and puuuuuuull back.
I get as horizontal as I can,
like   a   bug   gliding
along   the   surface.

The water likes that.
It lets me coast,
almost,
in the non-current.

After a few minutes,
I start to warm up.

A memory surfaces like a bubble—
Mom in her red Speedo,
hugging me tight on the pier,
only to drop me.
I am in the air,
then underwater,
    swallowing,
    sputtering,
    fighting to kick my way
    to the surface.
I am too surprised
to cry.

She laughs and reaches down a hand.
"Sink or swim, Tully.
It's the only way to learn."

I am shivering when she pulls me up,
with shock, not cold.
Her shoulder is warm.
She lets me bury my head in it.

"You're stronger than you know, kiddo,"
she whispers in my ear.
But when I lift my head,
she's looking at the water,
not me.

The memory sinks back down
under the surface, where it belongs.

I kick hard
once
to give myself a little push.
68 degrees isn't so bad
when you get used to it.
You can get used to anything
if you try hard enough.

The Godfather Swim

Sixteen minutes in
and I find my groove—
the lucky lane that's going to carry me
safely across 12.1 miles
of open water.

Plenty of people have done
the Godfather swim,
but none of them have been
as young as me.

It will be a record.
I will be a record breaker.

And Arch will get it all on film,
and we will post it everywhere
so Mom will see me succeed
at the plan that was ours
but is now just mine.

She'll have to return then
to make the victory ours again.

I've never seen the movie *The Godfather*.
Dad said it was too bloody.
Mom said it was too boring.

Violence doesn't bother me—it's all special effects.
But dullness does.

They call it the Godfather swim
because there is a huge mansion
across the lake
that was in one of the movies.
It's where I will touch land
at the finish line.
Finite.
The end.
Roll credits.

Because I am a minor,
what I am doing is not allowed
without adult supervision,
but my adults are otherwise occupied
with their own personal dramas,
which leaves it up to me and Arch
to do what needs to be done.

A marathon swim
isn't for the weak of heart
or mind.
It is 95 percent mental.
Sure, it's physical too,
but with hours of silence,
it's your head that will sink you
                              if you let it.

Sometimes the head plays tricks
that the body doesn't catch
until it's too late
and you've sabotaged your own self.

You start to imagine things in the water—
strange shapes beneath you,
a slick flick across your wrist,
a cold current,
a shimmering light,
a shore where there should be none.

And then you flip out,
literally.
You forget how to pull with your arms
and push with your legs
and when to turn your head to breathe,
because all you can think about is
what's real and what's not,
and that's when most swimmers
tap out,
call it quits.

With enough practice,
anyone can handle physical pain,
but no one wants to feel haunted.

That's what Arch is for—to shake me out of my head
and remind me what's real.
Arch is the most solid person I know.

It's why he's my best friend
and the only support crew (in water or on land)
that I would ever trust.

He reminds me that there are no lake monsters
or phantom lights.
He always points to shore.
But even Arch cannot shake off the tricks my mind plays
when it comes to the past or the future.

I'm starting to lose her.
She is
 a flash of red swimsuit,
 the oat-sweet scent of lotion,
 a barking laugh on a crowded street
 that I can never catch up to
   unless I win.

If I make this swim
and become the first and youngest marathoner,
then she will come back.
If . . . then.
Even she has to obey the universal laws of action and result.
She *has* to.
No one leaves a winner
at the top of her game.

The Godfather was fiction,
but this swim is my reality,
and it's going to bring my mother back.

Two Kinds

"Got the bell?" I shout to Arch,
who is still
orienting himself
on the open water
now that the shore has disappeared.

He digs into the supplies by his feet,
holds up the copper bell
that has traveled with me
to every swim I have swum,
only to be rung
if I win,
which will be today.

He wobbles a little
and almost loses his paddle
as he tucks it away again.

It's not that Arch is uncoordinated
or clumsy
or unathletic.
It's that there are two kinds of people in Tahoe:
Indoor People
                and
                      Outdoor People.

We all wear Keens
and weatherproof jackets,

but only some of us use them for
hiking
  biking
    skiing
      swimming
        kayaking
          trail-blazing
            heart-bursting adventuring.

Arch?
A successful Saturday is:
doing the mini crossword puzzle in the *New York Times*
over a bowl of Frosted Cheerios,
followed by a marathon of *American Pickers*,
and then more Frosted Cheerios
until I drag him out of the house
to breathe fresh air
before he disappears in his shed
for the rest of the day
to take apart junk
and put it back together again
into something new.

Dad is an Indoor Person too,
typing numbers and symbols on a black screen
at the desk in his office,
which overlooks the water,
though he never looks.

Instead, he types and taps and hits return
until he sits back, satisfied,

runs a hand over his shaved head, and says,
"The magic of code."
I point to the window
framing the pale outline of mountains and say,
"The magic's out there."

The Before and After

Dad doesn't listen
like he used to
BEFORE.

Before Mom left,
he would bike to the Swiss Mart with me,
king-sized Twix bars melting between our fingers
while we sat on the curb in the sun.
("Shhhh, don't tell Mom.")

Before she left,
he would tape the picture
from the "Memeing of Life" daily calendar
to my bathroom mirror.
(Grumpy Cat—"Have a nice day.")

But now,
in the AFTER,
he hides behind his screen,
typing in a secret language
only computers understand
because he can't face a world without Mom.

Me?
I like a good sunburn
    sore calves
    chapped lips

cracked hands
tight lungs.

I speak the language of the body
because that is what I am now—
a body pushing hard, harder, hardest,
until I reach the shore.

This past spring,
in my own AFTER,
school days were the worst—
I was trapped inside
like the birds
that fly into our garage in winter
and beat their wings against the shelves
because they cannot figure out
how they ended up in *this* place
when *their* place is so obviously
outside.

Every Saturday,
I woke up with the taste of freedom—
no class and no walls
for *two whole days*,
my mind ready to find
that blissful blankness
of forgetting
Mom.

The second I got out of bed I had to

MOVE
before the hurt caught up to me.

So I
trained in the water and on land—
running, resistance, weights—
until my heart was about to burst.

Better to burst with life
than sadness.

But the hurt always slammed into me in the end,
like a sucker punch from the universe.
She was gone.

I'd be icing my shoulder,
chilly drops trickling down my arm,
and *wham*,
she was gone.

I'd make a smoothie the wrong way,
too much banana,
not like Mom does it,
and *wham*,
she was gone.

I'd find her ChapStick
in the kitchen drawer,
the waxy taste of cucumber so familiar,
and *wham*,

she was gone.

The sun has fully risen now.
Orange arrows of light sparkle across the blue of the lake.
Dad can't hide forever,
and I'm done getting beaten up by the past.
I'm bringing her back
so we can all get on with our lives.

Today I chase the sun.

The Bell

The copper
bell dates all
the way back to third grade,
when Arch was learning to weld.
Most parents wouldn't hand a blowtorch
to a child. But most dads are not like Arch's,
who willingly sticks his body under ten tons of
heavy machinery, fixing cars every day. And most
moms aren't like Arch's, who runs the office at the
repair shop and can change a tire in under a minute.
Arch might be an indoor kid, pale and red-cheeked in
cold and heat, but they taught him how to hold his own
and his own is in the art of fire and metal. The bell was an
experiment. It all began with a piece of copper gutter Arch
found at the dump and ended with several cut fingers, but
also a triangular bell with a penny for a clapper that sounds
like a coin rattling around in a can when you shake it. He has
made better ones since—bigger ones with deeper pitches and
smoothed-out edges that you don't have to risk your digits to
handle. But *this* one—this bumpy, jagged, tinkling test run of
a contraption—became a lucky bell. It has come to every one
of my swim meets and every open-water adventure. There is
only one rule, instituted by my mom: "You don't ring it unless
you're FIRST, because the best things in life are *earned*." Today
I will ring that bell because I *will* be first: the youngest to swim
the marathon, just like Mom promised when we began to hatch
this plan a year ago. Except today it is Arch who carries the bell
instead of her. It is also Arch who will film and post the win on
all my channels where Mom is listed as a follower. More loyal
there than in real life. I give Arch a thumbs-up for the camera
and for my mother.

No Biggie

"Time!" I call.
"6:36!" Arch responds.

I perform a mental body check:
1. Head clear.
2. Skin on my shoulders warm from the sun.
3. Favorite yellow swim goggles holding steady.
4. Matching yellow swimsuit not rubbing or pinching.

All systems go, I think, and smile
at the idea of myself as a machine,
circuits buzzing with unstoppable energy.

I am a little over a twelfth of the way
according to Arch's GPS,
and all signs point to success
if I do it right.

I cup the water with my palms to glide forward,
and a tiny tremor runs down my hand.
My smile falters.

Yesterday I got a paper cut.

I was opening the mail,
hoping for a letter from Mom,
and then hating myself a little
when the hope dropped

like a rotten plum
at the sight of only bills and junk.

She wouldn't even take the time to type an email.
What made me think she'd pick up a pen?

I cut my finger on a DSW coupon—
"$10 off any $50 purchase"
sliced right through the tender pad of my thumb.

I wrapped it in toilet paper
and then a Cinderella Band-Aid.
It only bled a little.

No biggie, right?

Wrong.
An open wound in open water *is* a biggie.

I can feel it now,
that small flap of skin wriggling in the water,
free of its bandage.
(Disney princesses don't hold up in the elements.)

There's no salty sting because
Lake Tahoe is freshwater—
    runoff from the mountains
    that form the rim
    of the cup we're in.

No salt,
no sharks,
no sneaky vampire creatures
smelling blood and trailing me,
but . . .

I found an article in *Outside* magazine
when I was supposed to be researching
King Tut.

Hiding behind my orange binder,
under the radar of Mrs. Robinson, the librarian,
I read about
a man who got
(cue freaky *Jaws* theme song:
duuuun-dun
duuuun-dun
dun-dun
dun-dun
duuuuuuuuuun-dun)
eaten by flesh-eating bacteria.

Well,
not all of him.
It wasn't like he lost a limb.

He cut his ankle on a rock,
went to the doctor,
and got a shot.

No biggie, right?

Except when he went home
from swimming in this reservoir in Maine,
he got achy with
    chills and a fever,
    bone-crushing pain.

He went back to the doctor,
who looked at the cut
again
and found,
instead of blood and skin,
a whole colony of bacteria
feasting on his flesh.

Things grow on your body
in a body of water
that wouldn't find a home
otherwise.

As I dig in with my arms and pull
toward a shore I can't see,
it's thoughts like these
that make me go limp with fear.

You get a tiny cut
and think you're fine.
Your mom kisses you good night
and says, "We'll talk about it in the morning."

There are so many dangers you never see coming.

I shake my head,
take in a lungful of air,
and order myself to forget.

It's not the open water or the open wound
that'll get me in the end.
The mind is the biggest
danger of all.

My mother taught me that.

Playing by the Rules

"Two miles!" Arch shouts
to my left.

We are almost at the end of hour one.
I'm a little ahead of schedule.

I force my arms to slow,
my legs to drift,
my neck to relax,
so my heart will keep its steady
thu-thump.

The Godfather swim is not a sprint.
It is a long, slow trek that does not relent.

I follow a few blogs
of marathon swimmers—
all older than me, of course.
They give the same advice:
keep your heart steady
and your body loose.

Mind over matter is great and all,
but if your heart's skipping beats
and your legs are cramping,
your support crew is
going to

haul
you
out
before you ever see shore.

"Refueling for Tully Birch at 6:53 a.m.!"
Arch speaks into the camera.
A seagull overhead squawks in response.

I flip onto my back
as Arch passes me a banana
already peeled.
We are careful not to let our fingers touch.
That's a surefire way to get disqualified.

Support crew is never
ever,
ever
to touch the swimmer for any reason
ever.

The Lake Tahoe Open Water Swimming Association
loves its rules.
Here are a few more:
    1. Goggles and a swim cap and sunscreen are okay,
    but no wet suits.
    2. Support crew and boat are okay,
    but no catching a free ride in their current.
    3. Support swimmer is okay,
    but only for an hour at a time.

They are rules that might sound strange,
but everybody knows
you have to obey
if you want to play
the game.

We both know I will never get this chance again
because here are a few of their rules I *am* breaking:
1. Must have a guardian sign the waiver to acknowledge
the "extreme danger."
2. Must have a guardian accompany
the minor.
3. Must have a guardian . . .
4. Etc.
5. Etc.
6. Etc.
7. You get the idea.

I take a huge bite of banana,
so mushy from the open air I don't even have to chew,
and consider my support crew
stretching his back with the oar over his head
like he has just gotten out of bed.

There is no way Arch will get in and swim with me.
He was very clear on his responsibilities
when he agreed to this.

The Archibald Novak Swim Association rules are
much simpler:

1. He will:

> time me/feed me/talk to me.

2. He will not:

> swim with me/watch me struggle/abandon me.

And the minute I look like I'm about to lose it?

3. He will:

> call the coast guard/haul me onto his kayak/drag
> me home.

Which means I cannot lose it.

I'm playing the game,
but I have a secret.
I made a rule of my own:
I WILL NOT QUIT
(even if it's dangerous)
(even if it means losing my best friend).

HOUR TWO

Depression Is Spelled B-U-S-Y

Hour two.
Sixty-three minutes in.
If I wiggle with the timeline,
that's closer to one-third
of the way through
than not.

Tell *that* to my math teacher
who said I needed to work on my fractions.

Here's another fraction:
one antidepressant
reduced by half
each day
until
you
get
to
zero
will never get you to zero.

Half of half of half of half of half . . .
is still half.
There will always be a little bit left.
It's infinite steps toward infinity.

Which means

when my mom quit her medication
last January
ALL IN ONE GO,
she was just being practical,
right?

She created an end.

At least that's what she told my dad
out on the back deck
as they circled the patio table
mounded with snow
like squirrels ready for a fight.

But she was right.
She got herself to zero real quick.

No more lazy pancake breakfasts on Saturdays at IHOP.
No more weeklong games of Scrabble with me and Dad.
No more helping with my history project on Mesopotamia.

Instead, she . . .
left before sunrise to
run six miles on the lake trails
before
meeting her first patient at the
Sequoia Health and Aquatic Club,
where
she bent knees and rolled shoulders as a physical therapist,
then

coached my swim team, the Flippers,
until
we had to go home,
where
she ate dinner standing at the sink
while
doing a load of laundry
and
reading emails on her phone
and
half listening to me and Dad tell her about our days
so that
she could check us off her list
before
going to sleep
and
doing it all over again
tomorrow.

People say depression is:
    lying in bed
    not washing your hair
    losing your appetite
    crying all the time.

But for my mom, depression is:
never
ever
ever
ever
stopping.

I guess she ran in place so long
there was nothing left to do
but
leave.

Once Upon a Time

"Tully Birch,
I have been counting your strokes,
and you are ten-per-minute too fast.
SLOW DOWN!"

Arch puts away his bullhorn,
leans back in the kayak,
and squints at me.
Arch says more with a squint
than most people say all day.

I slow down.

It's . . . unpleasant.

My body is a dog on a leash,
and not just any dog—
a border collie
in a locked room,
gnawing at the doorframe,
craving release.

But I promised to let Arch hold the reins
(for now)
because even though my body wants to *go*,
my brain knows
that we have miles and miles

before we reach the shore.

Patience is a virtue
is a dumb saying.
But that doesn't make it untrue.

"Talk to me, Archibald.
If you're going to make me slow my roll,
you better provide some entertainment,"
I say between breaths.

He maneuvers closer to me
with a smooth paddle-stroke.
He might be an Inside Guy,
but he knows his way around the lake.

He pushes his sunglasses up higher on his head,
his dark hair shining blue-black
and cheeks pinkening in the sun.
He closes his eyes.
This is his thinking face.

My shoulders twitch,
seeking a harder pull,
but I force myself to keep pace with the kayak.
Arch lives to make me wait.

The water claps at my ears,
surging and sucking like the tide invading a cave.
But I roll over and do the backstroke,

lifting my head like a seal so I can listen.

"Once upon a time—"

"You can't start that way," I say.

"Why not?"

"Because I want something true."

"Who says a story that begins with 'once upon a time,'
can't be true?"

"Because they never are!"

He leans to his right,
tilting his boat and his body toward me
so he can give me a *look* before asking,
"How do you know?"

It's hard to roll my eyes in a swim cap,
but I manage.

He clears his throat.
"As I was saying,
once upon a time
there was a young couple
who lived peacefully
in the woods by a lake.

They thought they had everything they ever wanted—
　　a home that stayed warm in winter
　　and cool in summer,
　　fresh water to drink,
　　plenty of food to eat,
　　and a steady job fixing transport for all the villagers."

"The villagers," I snort.

He points his bullhorn at me.
"Don't interrupt a story before it's finished.
That's bad luck."

I could argue the many pluses of interrupting a bad story
and I would win,
but I can't afford to get Arch ruffled,
so I zip my lips
and signal Arch to keep going.

"The *villagers*," he repeats,
"paid the young couple well
for their services,
so that when they found out they were with child . . ."
He looks at me,
waits for a smart remark,
which it takes everything in my power not to make,
and then continues.
"When they found out they were with child,
they were overjoyed
and went out to celebrate

at their favorite local tavern."

"Aka Sonney's BBQ," I fill in.
He nods, and my stomach tightens
at the memory-scent of tangy vinegar fries
and the sound of crackling fat on a spit.
If all goes according to plan,
which it will,
the next four-and-a-half hours
are nothing but bananas
and PowerGels
and applesauce pouches.
My lips tighten against the cold bite
of lake water.

"Little did they know
that on their way back from this celebratory dinner,
on the winding, wet road
in the deepest dark of night,
destiny awaited."

Arch stills his paddle,
and without even meaning to,
my legs stop too.
I know exactly where this "fairy tale" is going.
We float together,
both itching for the best part of the story.

"Not far from home,
a car was parked

half-in,
　　half-out
of the road."

"Totally irresponsible," I add.

"Totally not their fault," he corrects,
"as is usually the case when you bust a tire.
And so the kindly gentleman—"

"Who fixes cars for a living," I insert.

"Who fixes cars for a living"—Arch grins—
"helped the city dwellers,
who knew nothing of tires or jacks or lug nuts,
get back on the road
toward their destination."

"Except!" I shout to the sky,
because it feels good to think of something happy
for a change.

"Except," Arch says,
"the Birches were very, very lost
and new in town
and also with child,
so the Novaks invited them into their home."

"And they lived happily ever after," I add,
then regret it,

because that's not how this story ends.

Arch is wrong.
Stories that start with *once upon a time*
are always fiction.
Reality is everything that happens
after.

The scariest thing
isn't a flat tire on a dark and rainy night.
It's the monster that lives in your head.
Mom taught me that.

Arch continues,
oblivious
to all the silty hurt
his story has stirred up
in my heart.

"And that's how our parents met,
making us best friends for life
before we were even born."
He sighs like you do after a satisfying meal.

I roll over,
cup my hands, and pull
HARD,
then scissor my legs
to catch the wake
I create.

He says something else after that,
but I don't catch it,
because I am already gone.

Break It Down for Me

Arch won an art contest
in fifth grade.
Any kid from any of the elementary schools
in the area could compete.
The winners got to display their project at the farmer's market
for the whole month of May.

The subject was:
"the importance of conservation of our natural resources."
Everyone else
    painted Mother Earth portraits,
    made water-bottle wind chimes,
    turned trash cans into flowerpots.

But Arch—
Arch collected hubcaps from his dad's shop,
weldedthemtogether,
and created a giant, six-foot-tall cockroach
with a Lexus symbol across its back
and radio antennae as, well, antennae.

The judge who gave him first prize
assumed it was a "condemnation of fossil fuels."
But Arch told me it was a big
GET OUT sign
to the tourists who ruin all the best hangout spots
around the lake.

Tahoe is an artsy town.

    Want to make handmade soap?

    Carved woodpeckers?

    Watercolor landscapes?

    Blown-glass chandeliers?

    Freshly fired pottery?

    Local sourdough?

    Beeswax lip balm?

Tahoe's your town.

Unless you're a kid.

If you're a kid,
you better know how to—

    lace a hiking boot

    wax a ski

    roll a kayak

    wrap a hockey stick

    start a fire

    clean a cut

or else.

Somebody stole the first-prize blue ribbon Arch taped
to his locker.

Arch is a man ahead of his time,
a rebel with a cause
that few people our age understand.

He's good at breaking things down into basic components
and then putting them back together
to make them better.
But he still lost his blue ribbon.

Because you can't mold a person's attitude
into the shape you want,
no matter how hard you try.

One time,
not long after Mom went off her meds last winter
I asked her if we could go skiing,
just the two of us.

"You bet, T,"
she said, and grabbed our skis.

We were on the mountain
in under an hour,
because when Mom wants to make something happen,
it does.

But halfway down our first run,
I lost sight of her silver ski suit
in the fresh powder, soft spun like cotton candy.

"Mom!" I yelled
until I was hoarse,
until people were staring,

until I had to sit down
because my legs were shaking.

It wasn't that I was scared or didn't know my way down.
It was that I didn't want to leave her
in case she was waiting,
in case she was wondering,
in case she was worried.

But I couldn't sit there forever.
So I lifted my goggles,
scraped away the tears,
and coasted down on wobbly legs.

When I got to the bottom,
she was sitting on a bench
in front of a café by the lift,
blowing on a cup of coffee.

She looked up when I called,
her sunglasses reflecting two of me, and said,
"Well, there you are."

Arch never reported the theft of his blue ribbon.
He said it wouldn't make a difference,
because whoever it was
had already settled on an opinion
of him,
and frankly

he did not
care enough
to change it.

I'm not trying to change Mom's brain
with this swim.
I just want to grab hold of her attention,
be a blip on her screen,
long enough for her to
remember me.

Alcatraz

Mile three
doesn't mean a thing.

Mile three might as well be mile six
when it comes to the murky middle
of a twelve-mile trek.

Trek—
otherwise known as a
     journey
               slog
                    trudge.

I am in the slog part of my trek,
where I can't see the start
or the finish,
so I have to keep
plodding along without letting myself think
how much
I have left
to go.

It was Mom who first saw the open water
as something to conquer.

A day at the beach
is never a day at the beach for her.

She is not a
    lie on your towel,
    read a paperback,
    sip on some lemonade
    with your sunshade up
kind of person.

My first open-water swim
was one mile.
Like a ruler, it was
"safe and measurable," Mom said.
"—a contained amount
you can see in your mind
and feel in your body," Mom promised.
(I was terrified.)

Six years old,
bony knees shaking
but jaw jutting out
to prove I was tough
for the one-mile swim
from the San Diego Convention Center
to the Tidelands Park beach
at the foot of the Coronado Bridge.

Mom swam next to me,
red swimsuit and tanned arms
flashing in and out of the waves
as she shouted,
    "Go, Tully, go!"

"Dig in, T!"
"I'm so proud of you!"

I would have swum
to the moon
to hear those words.

I won first place.

After I jumped off the plastic crate
that was the makeshift podium,
she picked me up
and squeezed me tight, tight, tighter
than she'd ever squeezed—
like a favorite stuffed animal
you thought was lost
until you spied
it under the bed.

I lifted my medal up high
so it was over both our heads.

That was the beginning.

We took Alcatraz when I was nine.
Three miles from Aquatic Park to the Rock and back.
Remember,
three miles is nothing,
right?

Except those three miles were everything.

From the start,
that swim was different.
The weather was bad—
    heavy clouds
    gusty wind
    slanting rain
    with a creeping chill
    that sank into my bones.

"You sure you want to do this, kiddo?" Dad asked,
his glasses fogged from breathing into his hands.
I looked to Mom, who was watching the water,
her eyes the same cool gray as the waves.

She did not say "go" or "stay."
She didn't have to.

I pulled my goggles on
and my warm-up pants off
and walked to the water's edge.

I could feel Mom behind me,
then beside me,
our thighs covered in goose bumps
but neither one of us shivering,
like our bodies knew what would come next
would be much worse.

From the beginning,
the tide was a bully,
pushing me around,
 trying to make me quit,
 trying to pull me back,
 trying to keep me from "my potential,"
 as Mom likes to say.

The waves in the bay were fierce,
but we were fiercer.

When I pushed my way through,
like a kid in a crowded hall,
Mom shot me a thumbs-up and smiled,
her lips blue-purple like a bruise from the cold.

I gave her my own bruised smile back.

After the first leg,
I settled in and
hit my stride
like I am now
in the lake,
which is mercifully calm.
It wants me to win.
It is not a bully
like the bay.

We made it to Alcatraz and back
in a little under

three hours.
I was forty-eight pounds,
the smallest in my category,
and the only girl.

I took first.

Afterward
we went for pizza at a place off North Point
with a bunch of other families from the swim.
Dad kept feeling my hands,
checking to see
if I had warmed up again.
But Mom was quiet,
picking pepperonis off her slice
and stacking them like plates.

All the energy that had pushed her in the race
had leaked out—
left in the water at the base of the Rock.
Once the challenge was done,
there was nothing left to hold her up.

She had a name for this mood
when it claimed her—
"Blue Period."
I was just learning to write
when she first came up with that.
I imagined it as a period at the end of a sentence,
neat and round.

But that's not what it is.
It is a big, gaping hole
that you can't see coming
or know when it ends.

During one of Mom and Dad's fights on the deck,
where they went to yell and pace
and pretend a pair of sliding glass doors
was soundproof,
I heard Mom call her depression
"a prison in my mind."

"Prison" is a much better name than "Blue Period"
in my opinion.
I would have told her that
if she'd asked.

That day at Alcatraz,
I shivered when I reached the rocky shore
of the former prison
and raced back as fast as I could.

That night over pizza,
I slipped my medal
under the table
and into her palm.
Briefly,
she smiled.

I was only nine,

but I would do anything
to help Mom
escape.

Two Clocks

"Uh, Tully?"
Arch steers the kayak closer
until there is less than a paddle's length
between us.
He holds up his phone in its waterproof case—
the phone that has been recording
my record breaking.

Except that's not what it's doing right now.

Right now,
it is receiving a call . . .
from my dad.

My arms falter,
and I stop midstroke.

Why is he calling?
It's Saturday morning,
not even nine.
His days don't start like mine.
He should still be groggy with sleep
and fumbling for his glasses
on the bedside table,
where I strategically left a note
explaining that I would be at Arch's
so he didn't need to worry.

"What did you tell your parents?"
I ask, half expecting
to see Dad
cutting through the water
in our rickety fishing boat.

Arch's arm wobbles,
and droplets from the paddle
speckle my goggles.
"What you told me to tell them.
That I was with *you*."

The phone lights up again
with another call,
and we stare at it
like it's a bomb.

"Don't answer it!" I hiss,
then spit water
as my chin
dips below a wave
caused by a passing yacht.
We are not alone on this lake.
I pray one of those boats
isn't my dad.
If it's a yacht,
it's most definitely not.

The phone stops ringing.
Arch carefully tucks it into the pocket of his life vest.

I take three deep breaths
to stretch my tightening chest
and to remind myself to breathe.
Then I kick off again.

There were always two clocks
on this marathon swim.
One started when I left shore.
The second started when Dad realized I am not
where I claimed
to be.
I hoped I'd be closer to the finish line
when that happened.

"Check the GPS.
Make sure we're still heading northwest."

Arch salutes me
with a shaky hand.
He does not like this one bit.
He tells his parents everything
because he does not have parents like mine.

His dad is big and loud,
with fingernails black from motor oil
no matter how many times Arch's mom
reminds him to scrub.
He smells like Irish Spring soap,
and his coveralls are extra-soft from so many washings.

His mom is compact and round,
with long, gray hair
that does not match her smooth face,
which only wrinkles
when she laughs,
which she does often.
She smells like the lavender she grows in her garden
and tucks in her dresser
between her sweaters,
which are stretched and nubby
and covered in patterns that remind me of tropical birds.

They eat dinner in front of the TV
because they got home so late from the car shop
where he manages the cars
and she manages the books.
They talk all the way through their favorite crime dramas,
and Arch's mom makes the best
Tater Tots casserole with extra tots
that I have ever had.

Dad and I sit at the table
and do meatless Mondays
like they say you're supposed to.
But we don't talk
or laugh
since Mom has gone.

Here's a thing I would never say out loud:
sometimes I wish I could be part of Arch's family—

a Novak through and through
with hand-knit, shaggy sweaters
and dirt under my nails
and a house lined with wind chimes,
a house that smells of cooking meat and onions
and spills over with laughter
at all the commercial breaks.

If Dad knew what I was up to today—
    crossing the lake
    to break a record
    without adult supervision
    after the worst year of our lives—
he would say,
"Acting out your anger
with risky behavior
is not going to solve anything,"
because he loves to quote Anil, the therapist
who he makes me see
but won't see himself.

He doesn't get it.
He never has.
This isn't anger.
This is *anticipation*.

If I can really do this,
it will be the big win,
the *biggest* win,
that Mom will *have* to see

when she remembers that this swim
was supposed to be
for us.

She'll pick up her phone
just to check,
just to check,
and when she does,
it will shake her
out of the worst Blue Period yet.

Who needs therapy
when you have the lake
and a record to break?

"If the phone rings again,"
I call to Arch
while smoothing out my swim cap,
"don't answer it."

HOUR THREE

Forecast Highly Variable

I lob the empty applesauce pouch
into the kayak,
where it lies flat like a sunbather on a dock,
except . . .

There is no sun.

That early-morning sunrise
that caused the lake to shimmer
peach and coral and cream
has grown dimmer.
The lake
mirrors something else now,
something darker.

I glance up at the sky.
A thick cloud sits
in front of the sun
like a troll
at the entrance to a cave.

I flip onto my back and scan the horizon,
where a trail of troll clouds dutifully follows
toward my lake
on *my* day
during the most important swim of
my life.

"Check it, Arch,"
I order.

He does not have to ask what I mean.

I'd feel bad for bossing him around,
except he does the same to me
when we are in his shed,
surrounded by his art.
That's his territory.
The lake is mine.

Living in a lake-and-mountain town
is a lot like being a sailor at sea—
the weather isn't a conversation starter;
it *is* the conversation.

He retrieves the dry bag,
which holds anything we cannot afford to get wet.
He opens his phone, begins to type.

"30 percent chance at ten.
48 percent chance at eleven."
He frowns at his phone
like it has wronged him.
It has wronged us both.

Back in Arch's shed,
at the edge of his property,

where he keeps

    scraps of metal

    old bumpers

    discarded tires

    bent road signs

    safety goggles

    a welding torch

    a backpack full of Goldfish and peanut butter crackers,

there is a bulletin board.

Pinned to that bulletin board
is the twelve-mile route from Cave Rock
to the Grand Avenue Dock,
and under that
is a chart of the average sunrises and sunsets in Tahoe
in July,
and under that
is a list of the average water temperatures of the lake in July,
and under that
is a graph of the weather patterns.

We knew to meet a little before six,
right as the sky began to lighten.
We knew the water would be cold but bearable.
We knew what path to take and what fuel to pack.
But we could only guess
how the weather would behave.

We checked the ten-day forecast and picked a date
and prayed to the weather gods to bless our journey

across the water.
But the sky
is turning gray.
And the waters
are losing their shine.
Hope flickers
in the finicky wind.

The phone rings in Arch's hand.
I am guessing it is not the sun
calling to tell us not to worry.

Arch holds it up.
I wipe the specks from my goggles to check
what I already know:
Dad.
Dad.
Dad.
Dad.
And Arch's mom.
So many missed calls
that are getting closer together,
like the clouds overhead
and the pressure building in my chest.

Forget keeping a pace.
I dig in hard,
put my head down,
and swim
like I am being chased.

The forecast is grim,
but I can't get in my head again.

I focus on form:
strong lines
down my back,
top to toe.
I am an arrow
flying toward its target.

I will outpace the storm *and* Dad.

Bubbles

Above the waterline,
Arch shouts something
about time.
But I keep my head down
because underwater
there is no storm.
There is only
blanket-thick silence
drawn over my head,
safe and a little smothering.

Air whooshes out from my nose,
and Morse-code blips of bubbles float up
    past my goggles
    toward a surface
    that is not
    so calm and quiet
    as this.

I used to love bubbles,
the kind you'd get in a tiny bottle as a favor
at every birthday party.

I loved the slippery feel of the soapy water
sliding between my thumb and index finger
as I fished around in the bottle
for the wand.

I loved the rainbow swirl of colors
that twirled on the tip of the loop
when I finally pulled it out
to study potentially the best bubble
of my life.

But what I loved *most*
was the moment right after I blew
    a whisper-breath
    across the air
    so gently
and watched the circle grow and grow,
shifting shapes,
stretching long and thin,
then wide and round,
until it was as big and beautiful
as it was going to get.

That was my moment—
the split second before it wasn't my bubble anymore,
when it would either pop
or leap into the world on its own
to float wherever it wanted to go.

Dad loves bubbles too.

One summer we performed an experiment:
we made ten different bubble solutions
in various degrees of soapiness,
and we bought ten different wands

in various shapes and sizes,
and we lined them up along the deck rail
to test them out.

It took all day
because we had to test them in different wind conditions
and because I spilled the soap
at least four times.
Dad didn't care.
He smirked and shrugged and said,
"This deck has never been cleaner."

Mom watched through the glass
of the patio door
while she sipped her coffee and stretched
after her morning run.
She didn't join us.

She didn't have the patience for the time it took
to stop and plot the results
on the chart we made
on the big piece of butcher paper
Dad let me tape to the deck.

Blowing bubbles
always reminds me
that what I'm doing matters,
even if it doesn't last.

Wrong Way Out

There is a twitch in my left calf
that does not hurt
but does not help either
when I'm trying to keep a pace
that is definitely too fast for mile six
but maybe too slow,
even now,
to beat the storm.

Several fishing boats and a few pontoons
are already turning
back to shore.
Their wakes
create a choppy cross-stitch
of waves
that makes it almost impossible
for me to swim
    in
          a
straight
    line.

I rub the cut on my thumb.
Is it worse or just my imagination?
I picture bacteria
like an evil Pac-Man,
chomping on the raw flesh around the scabbed edges.

I'm too inside my body.
Every twitch and tickle and cramp
registers as a glitch in my brain
that shoots panicky adrenaline
straight to my heart,
which is not holding steady
with all these outside forces
closing in.

I need my body to be a machine,
but instead, all I can think is . . .
My shoulders burn,
    which is normal,
but the pain doesn't stop
when I coast for a few strokes,
    which is not.

I would not be out of shape
if it weren't for Mom.

She quit her job
at the Sequoia Club
less than twelve hours before she skipped town.

When she left,
all I could feel was
                her absence.
The hurt was so big
nothing else got in,
like when I hold my face too close to my phone

and the picture dissolves into colors and dots.
All I saw and felt was
    her hair tie on the kitchen table,
    her muddy trail shoes in the garage,
    her favorite cinnamon-raisin oatmeal
    that nobody else likes
        sitting half-eaten
        in a bowl
        in the sink
        like she would be back any minute.

But then,
when a day turned into two
and a week turned into a few,
life yanked me away from the close-up,
and I began to notice all the *other* losses
her leaving opened up,
fresh as potholes in the road after melting snow.

We couldn't go to the farmer's market on Saturdays
because too many people stopped us
to ask where Mom was.

We didn't ride our bikes to breakfast on Sundays
because the tires were low
and Mom was the only one
who knew where we kept the pump.

And biggest of all—
we couldn't afford to pay the club fees at Sequoia

without Mom's salary and employee discount,
so I had to quit the swim team.

When Dad told me that,
I yelled and threw his favorite
Guardians of the Galaxy coffee cup
off the deck and into the woods.
It wasn't at all satisfying
and not just because it didn't break,
but because the person I really wanted to scream at
wasn't there.

So instead of training with Mom
for the biggest swim of my life,
I had to do it
on my own
whenever I could sneak out,
which was nearly impossible
with a dad who works from home.

But I did the best I could—
going to Arch's house after school,
swimming the length of shore along Cave Rock,
the Lady of the Lake watching me
instead of my mother.

Arch was my timekeeper,
and we clocked as many hours as we could
before a parent called us to come back from
"the library,"

where we were
"doing work."

I hold my nose and blow a frustrated burst of air
to clear my ears.
All that training still wasn't enough,
because here I am
feeling the ten-mile burn
at mile six.

There's nothing left to do but keep digging.

A ski instructor once told me
that if you are ever caught in an avalanche,
the greatest danger
is that you lose your sense of
UP   DOWN.
                and
People try to dig
the wrong way out.

The trick, he said,
was to cry or spit
to see which way it falls,
and then you know the way up.

93 percent of avalanche victims survive
if rescued in the first fifteen minutes.
But after that, the number
drops.

I bend my heel
to stretch my twitchy calf
and wonder—
what's Mom's time limit?

It's been four months.

How fast do I have to be
before she's so far sunk
in her depression
that she doesn't want
to be pulled back
to the surface?

And then a worse thought bubbles up . . .
What's my time limit
before I don't care?

Things We Don't Talk About

I look over at Arch,
paddle resting on his lap,
water drip, drip, dropping from the yellow tip
while he squints at his phone
with his sunglasses propped on his forehead,
which is wrinkled in worry.

Or maybe he just can't see the screen.
Because Arch does not worry.
He lets life unwind
like a kite on a string.

Me?
I let loose a teensy bit,
and my life unravels
like a favorite sweater
that will never be
the same again.

He huffs and jams the phone into the dry bag.
Arch also doesn't get angry.
Something wriggles inside me—
a worm of regret.

On April 3 of last year,
the school ran a food drive
because that's the kind of people-loving place

we claim to be:
"Bring your cans of soup, bags of beans,
boxes of mac and cheese,
but leave the perishables at home, please!"
We like to help.
We recycle.
We wash our hands with environmentally friendly soap.
We love the earth and everyone on it.

Except on April 3,
Brent from math class
thought it would be funny
to deface/defame/degrade (see, I pay attention in English)
Arch's food-drive poster.

The sharp alcohol scent of permanent marker stung my nose
before I even heard the squeak-drag of the pen
across the paper pinned next to the cafeteria.

It was followed by snickers of sneaky laughter,
which is how I knew whatever Brent
had written would leave a mark
more lasting than pen.

By the time I got to them,
Brent's little group had loosened their circle
enough for me to view the damage.

They had given the earth a name—
"Arch."

Its smiling face now had
thick glasses perched
on a nose oozing boogers
into a braces-filled mouth,
with an arrow
pointing down
like an axe
waiting
to
fall.

Below it, Brent had written,
"Save the planet! Lose this waste of space!"

Arch's mom says bullies are boring
and there's no new insult under the sun,
so don't let it get to you.
I say life's hard enough
and we are all bodies trying not to bump into
one another,
so let everybody do their own thing
and leave them alone.

But I did not leave Brent alone on April 3.
On April 3, I gave Brent a gentle shove,
which just so happened to cause him to trip,
because Brent's ego is so big
it makes him lose his balance.

He might have said a few choice words.
I might have said a few back.

Principal Blackburn may have gotten involved,
and I may have been suspended two days.

On the night of the incident,
after Mom lectured me for jeopardizing
my swimming career
while Dad shifted his feet behind her,
Arch called.

"Hey, Archibald, what's up?"
I said with a smile in my voice.

"None of your business,"
he said with a frown in his.

"What's that supposed to mean?"
I thought he'd be proud!
I defeated the villain!
I became the hero
he's always telling me I am.

"It means don't start a fight
that I have to finish!"

I got up off my bed.
This was not a conversation to have
lying
down.

"Did he mess with you after I left?" I asked,
the familiar rush of anger pumping in my ears.

"No, he didn't *mess with me*!" Arch growled back,
"Because I avoided him
and everybody else
the rest of the day.
I ate lunch on the stage in the gym in the dark
thanks to you."

"But that's the problem, isn't it?" I hissed.
"You never *fight*.
They poke at you for your art.
They poke at you for being smart.
They pokepokepoke
and you never *do* anything!"

"So *what*?"
The words echoed off the metal walls
of his shed out back,
where I could just picture him pacing—
alone in the dark
again.
"You don't get to decide what I do!
You don't get to decide what I let bother me!"

Arch was ruining all my Brent anger,
so it morphed into a new grabby monster aiming for Arch.
"How can it *not* bother you?!"

"Because I'm not like you!
I don't wake up wanting to punch the world in the face!"
He paused.
The crack of silence
filled up like a glass under the tap
with his sadness and madness
at a problem that was not mine
and should never have been.
My whole body went limp.

"I'm sorry, Arch."

"Yeah," he said, and sighed and hung up,
and that was the last time he ever mentioned it.
By the time I got back from my suspension,
the food drive was over
and all the posters were gone.

I watch him tuck his phone away now
over swirling gray-green waters.
He holds out his paddle
to pass over my peanut-butter pouch.

We do not talk about the storm
or the hours we have left until we reach shore
or the kind of trouble we will be in when we get there,
just like we do not talk about April 3.

I have dragged him into another fight

he did not want to be in,
and now I don't know how to say sorry
without saying I was wrong.

The Family Motto

Mother Nature gives me a break
at the end of mile six.

The clouds part,
and the sun shakes out her golden hair,
scattering light and heat
across my shoulders/neck/back.

The warmth sinks into my bones
and zings my energy back up to 100 percent,
like I've been plugged in
to recharge.

"Arch!" I call,
"I'm bored! Tell me another story!"

"Only you would get bored
trying to break a world record!"
he shouts back.
But he picks up the bullhorn
and clears his throat,
just as relieved as I am
that we dodged
the storm
at least for now, I think,
and then hate myself for thinking it
because I have to stay *positive*!

That's what Mom always said
when I was two strokes behind
and nearing my last lap.
"It's not over until somebody touches the wall!"
she'd yell over the whoosh of water
and rush of cheering crowds.

I flip over
and do the backstroke
so I can hear him better
and drown out my own thoughts
as he begins.

"Once upon a time—"

"I'm sensing a theme here—"

"Don't interrupt,
or I will turn this kayak around right now,
young lady," he replies.

He'd do it too.
I zip my lips.

"Once upon a time,
in the village where our two heroes meet,
there was a great snowstorm
that covered the tiny hamlet
so completely that

it sealed it from the rest of the world
like a—"

"Snow globe!" I shout,
because I love snow globes
and have a collection
of all the places
I have competed,
from San Diego to San Antonio.

"Exactly like a snow globe." Arch nods.
"Nothing got out and nothing got in.
For a whole week,
travelers stayed away,
schools closed,
and the villagers got to play
on their own mountain
like it was a winter wonderland
built just for them,
because for seven days,
it was."

I remember the week from this past January
when an ice storm
slicked the roads
and then four feet of snow followed.

Arch's parents' shop was slammed with cars
wrecked from the weather.

They worked overtime
while the rest of Lake Tahoe
    made snowmen
    went snowshoeing
    rode the chairlifts with no lines
    skied the fresh powder with no crowds
    ate at all the fancy restaurants without a reservation.

"Like a kid after three ICEEs at the pool," Arch continues,
"the town was whipped into a frenzy
at having the place to themselves."

"But—" I say,
because I know what's coming.

"But," Arch adds, rowing closer
so that I have to be careful not to accidentally
brush the side of the kayak.
What a way to get disqualified—
accidental contact during story time.
"Our two heroes knew
that a few of the youngest villagers
were trapped,
held captive by the snow
(and their parents).
They needed OUT, and there were only two people
who could rescue them.
So Lady Tully and Lord Arch—"

"Nope."

"Lord Tully and Lady Arch?"

I flick him with water. "Try again."

"How about Sir Tully and Sir Arch?
That way we can be knights."

"Deal."
I nudge ahead of him,
using all my fully charged muscles
to sneak up the pace
while Arch is distracted.

"Sir Tully and Sir Arch
raided both their garages
and those of their neighbors
to collect as many sleds as they could manage,
and with orange rope and yellow caution tape,
they marked off the
safest
snowiest
smoothest
hill they could find,
before gathering all the youngsters."

I snort at *youngsters*,
which makes me suck up water and cough.
I look back to catch Arch's that's-what-you-get-for-
mocking-me look.
He got it all on camera, of course.

"They made a list of all the *youngsters* in the neighborhood
whose daycares had been closed,
whose parents were busy working from home,
who couldn't be trusted outside alone,
so they spent their best snow days
pressing their noses to the glass
because no one would take them
to play.
Sir Tully and Sir Arch
broke them out."

Arch raises his paddle in remembered victory.

In *reality,*
it was a painful two hours of knocking on all the doors
and explaining to all the stressed-out parents
what we were going to do
and where we were going to be.
Worst community service ever,
but not to Arch.

About a decade ago,
his mom hung a hand-painted sign in their hallway
that reads:
"How can I be of service?"
It might as well be their family motto.

"Sir Tully and Sir Arch
trotted them over to the roped-off hill
and handed them borrowed sleds

on stolen time,
so they too could live
the best snow week of their lives,"
he says, satisfied with his retelling.

"And there was only one bloody nose,
when Maizie and her sister crashed into each other,"
I add.

Arch grins and lifts the bullhorn to his lips to shout,
"And with minimal bloodshed,
everybody lived happily ever after!"

I smile at him
and flip back over,
but once my face is safely hidden by the water,
I slip off the grin like a
wrong-sized flipper.

The story Arch told
is only half the truth.

Arch was being kind
letting me in on the action.
But it was all his idea.
Not that he would ever say that
because that's not the kind of person Arch is.
Not like me,
who always has to make sure everyone
sees my time lit up on the board during meets and

hears my answer in history class and
watches me race down the steep driveway
at school in my Rollerblades.

If I were a knight,
I'd demand they make
the round table
a rectangle
so I could sit at the head of it.
If our family had a motto, it would be:
"Every person for themselves."

The *real* reason I agreed to help
was because I did not want to be at home.
Mom hadn't left yet,
but we might as well have been camped
on top of a mountain of doom—
the air stretched so thin
it left you light-headed.
To be home was to be alone
with a dad who disappeared behind his computer screen
and a mom who disappeared behind her phone
and her exercise routine.
At least Dad was doing his job.
Mom was making a choice.

I didn't know it then,
but I was six weeks away
from her disappearing for good.

I wish I could go back
and sled forever
on a roped-off hill
where everything is safe
because I know
somebody is looking out
for me.

What's in a Name

During art class this year,
we had to look up our names
in a baby book
covered in pink writing and blue ABC blocks.

And then we had to draw a self-portrait
based on the definition
we were given
that showed whether we agreed
or disagreed
with the description.

"Tully" is my mother's maiden name.
According to the pink baby book,
my name means
"quiet" and "peaceful."

You can imagine what my mother said when I told her that.

She flicked the lip of her coffee cup
before pushing away the paper
on which I had written our name's definition
and said,
"Tully, you are the loudest, fiercest girl I know,
and you come from a long line of loud, fierce women.
Don't let anyone tell you otherwise."

And then we shared a sneaky-cat smile
because we had just
biked an extra three miles
even though her therapist
and Dad
said Mom had to slow down.

I loved doing something with Mom that was just for us,
but—
I hated keeping it a secret.
Can you love-hate something?
Or someone?

"Arch" comes from "Archibald,"
which means
"truly brave."
That one I can get behind.

Still,
I'm not sure you can flatten out a person
into words like that.

Arch made his self-portrait
out of metal.

I didn't make one at all,
because I am only
just learning who I want to be.

HOUR FOUR

The Best-Laid Plans

At almost 9:00 a.m.,
with 5.75 miles left of my swim,
the sun is still beating back the clouds,
and I am over halfway there.

BUT

Dad has stopped calling.
So has Arch's mom.
Silence is never good.
Silence means someone
is coming up with a plan B.

Plan B
could be . . .
Dad driving by Arch's place
to check for my Rollerblades by the front door,
but when he doesn't see them,
it would spiral
into a race to the auto shop,
where Arch's mom would tell him
that Arch said he would be with *me*
at *my* house,
which would lead to plan C.

Plan C
could be . . .

Dad hauling out the motorboat
and cruising the lake,
unless he's too panicked to drive,
which would lead to plan D.

Plan D
could be . . .
Dad calling the coast guard
and the coast guard sending out search boats,
or worse—
Dad calling the cops
and the cops deciding I am M-I-S-S-I-N-G.

I feel good right now,
rooted in my body in a way I haven't felt
since mile one.
I am not missing.
I am HERE and I am ALIVE!

Which means . . .
I cannot afford
any other option
but plan A,
the one I designed,
which is to finish this race,
post the video as proof
that I am the youngest marathoner to conquer
the Godfather swim,
and convince Mom,
who *is* missing,

that I am HERE and I am ALIVE
and I'm worth
showing up for.

I have to think like Mom—
be sneaky
to make sure what I want to accomplish
gets done,
like the kind of heroes who do good
undercover
so they can right the wrongs
the world is too scared or weak
to handle.

Which leads me to
the next step in plan A:
lie.

I breathe it out
on each exhale:
"Arch . . .
text . . .
your . . .
mom."

"What?!"
He whips around so fast he almost capsizes himself.
"Are you sure?"
I ignore the relief in his voice.

Shake my head
under the water,
where he can't see it.

"We have to stop them from freaking out. Tell her . . ."
I take a double-deep breath this time.
Lying is harder
when it's planned.
"Tell her I fell coming to your place, and . . .
and we went to Walgreens to get Band-Aids and stuff."

He purses his lips,
even as he types.
"They'll never believe it.
We have Band-Aids at home.
And you never fall."

He's right.
For once I wish
I'd been better
at being worse.

The phone buzzes in Arch's hand
immediately after he hits send,
and he almost drops it in the water.

"My mom says"—
he stops and groans—
"to call your dad."

I am out of breath
from trying to keep my head above water
and hold a conversation
for this long.

"Figure it *out*, Arch."

He narrows his eyes at me
and gives me one of his mother's looks—
the one that tells me I am seconds away
from ultimate elimination
from his good graces.

"Look . . ."
I pause,
trying to keep my tone even
when all I want to do is scream in frustration
for him to just
listen to me!
"Text him from your phone
but pretend to be me.
Tell him the same story and that we're going into town
to get some ice cream
or whatever.
Be *vague*."

That is the one key to lying that I *do* know.
Details get you caught.

"I don't think I—"

"Arch!
Just do it!"

His look could cut glass.

Everything stutters—
my stroke,
my heart,
my hope
that my world
hasn't fallen apart.

"Please, Arch," I beg.
"This was part of the bargain, remember?
When you swore to be my support crew?"

His whole body slumps
as he gives in,
but the doubt's still there,
like a shadow
hidden by a cloud.

At least for now,
we are a team again.

I duck back under,
leave him to deal with it,
and kick off toward
the next mile.

The Best Day of My Life

The worst day of my life
was the day after
the best day of my life.

The best day of my life
happened to be the regional swim meet
in which the Flippers, Sequoia's strongest team in history,
was predicted to dominate.

Mom took her job as physical therapist at the club seriously,
but she treated her job as our coach like it was a sacred oath,
and the number one thing she taught us was:
WE CAN DO HARD THINGS.

Some of those hard things included:
    Holding the plank position for one minute.
    Leg-and-arm lifts while lying on our stomachs.
    Breath holds.
    Wall squats.
    Hot yoga.

A few of the parents complained about the hot yoga.
"105 degrees in a box for ninety minutes is too much,"
they kept saying,
until we won district, and then
105 was just fine by them.

I miss a lot of things about swimming with the Flippers,
but I do not miss hot yoga,
where downward-facing dog
leaves the sweat
D
R
I
P
P
I
N
G
up your nose
and into your ears.

But on that day in March,
I would have done a thousand downward dogs in the hot box
if it would secure my qualification for state.

The meet took place in the sports complex north of the city.
The pool was Olympic-sized
but gritty,
with the crusty buildup of too much chlorine
along the edges.

Flags hung high
on the blue-painted walls
boasting the state winners
from all the way back
to 1976.

I wanted to see our team on that wall.

All of us were jittery with nerves,
jumping at the sound of referees' whistles
and bodies slamming into the plexiglass
as the hockey teams practiced
next door.

But Mom—
Mom chewed her spearmint gum
with her sunglasses down
and her arms crossed
while she studied the competition—
the Tritons, Tigers, Seahorses, and Tsunamis—
as they removed their warm-ups
and windmilled their arms
across the arena.

She caught me watching her
and lifted her glasses
to give me a wink.
And then she told me to fill up my balloon.

It isn't a real balloon.
It's a breathing exercise
to help you calm down
and stretch your lungs.

The best practice we ever had

was when she brought in real balloons
to help us learn.

Mine was purple.
I sat with my legs dangling in the water
and held the balloon in my arms
as Mom counted off.

We all breathed in deep,
like our chests were the balloons
filling up with air,
and then we pursed our lips
to let the air out
in little puff, puff, puuuufffffs
until our heart rates were steady.

At regionals that day,
I wrapped my towel around my neck
and did ten balloons
until I felt loose,
and all the worry
emptied out of me.

My strongest event is the hardest event:
the butterfly.
It sounds beautiful,
graceful even.
Picture a big, orange butterfly with black tips
flitting over the marigolds by the lake's edge.

But the real deal
in the water
is a different animal altogether.

Unlike the breaststroke or backstroke,
which are what I'm relying on now
to get me across these twelve miles of lake,
the butterfly uses all the core muscles at once.
You have to lift yourself *up* and *out* of the water
like,
well,
a butterfly.
You pretend you are flying
and you *LIFT*,
but that requires all the muscles in your
    arms
    shoulders
    stomach
    back
    legs
to *PUSH* at the same time.

"You're a bullet out of a gun," Mom whispered,
right before I took my place on the starting block
and shook out my hands
one last time.

In the stands, Dad wore a shirt
that said,
"Education Is Important, Swimming Is Importanter"

and help up a sign
that read,
"Keep Calm and Swim On."

I didn't hear the whistle
so much as feel it,
and then I was leaping

                    stretching

                        shooting

through the water—
a butterfly bullet.

I felt the other swimmers around me
fight the water,
like it was something wild to be tamed,
but I knew better.
I let the water carry me
so that we moved together
as a team.

When I touched the wall,
I knew before I looked
that I beat my record.
One for the books,
I could already hear Mom say.

But it still wasn't enough
to earn first.

I forced myself to smile on the podium,

and I cupped my second-place medal
like a broken heart in my hands.
Then I looked to Mom,
who had her sunglasses down
again.

In the locker room,
Mom gave a pep talk
about the upcoming state championship,
which we still qualified for
despite my second-rate finish.

She quoted Michael Phelps:
    "If you want to be the best,
    you have to do things
    that other people
    aren't willing to do,"
while I sat on the bench
in my damp swimsuit
and thought of all the things I did do:
    breathed my balloons
    became a bullet
    bested my best time
and the thing I didn't:
    beat the girl who came in first.

At least I also didn't cry.
We don't do that in our family.
But when I wiped my nose on my towel,
Mom noticed.

After the other girls filed out,
she sat down on the bench,
and I braced myself for a lecture
    about priorities
    about giving it my all
    about the extra sleep I snuck
    about the protein shakes I could never finish . . .

But she tucked a stray red wisp of hair
back into my ponytail
and said instead,
"Your personal best, T.
That means ice cream for dinner."
And then she hugged me,
which she never does,
so it took me a second to hug her back.
When I did,
I didn't want to let go,
ever.

I held on as long as I could
even though I was getting her track jacket all wet.
She broke away first.

And then me and Mom and Dad went out for banana splits
(which she never lets us eat).
    I ate all I could stomach—
    three scoops of ice cream,
    aaaaaaall the nuts, hot fudge, and cherries
    because she said it was a celebration.

Head throbbing with the rush of cold
and veins thrumming with sugar,
I smiled into my empty dish.
BEST. DAY. EVER.

I should have remembered—
she didn't let me ring the bell.

The Worst Day of My Life

The worst day of my life started out in the dark—
that middling part of night
when it is impossible to tell whether
you are closer to evening
or morning.

A hand shook me awake
at 1:03 a.m.
I shot up and almost fell out of bed.
There'd been wildfires in the area,
the smoke hanging low like fog over the lake.
I thought our house was going up in flames.

But it was Mom,
sitting by my feet,
fully dressed in running gear.

She smiled at me
with her usual smile,
and the salty sweet taste
of our banana splits
came back to me.
For months before that,
ever since she
    went off her meds,
    stopped seeing her therapist,
    upped her hours at the club,

her smile had been a flattish line.
Tonight it quirked up at the end.
I felt lucky.

"Hey, T,
want to go on an adventure?"
she whispered.

I looked at the clock
and rubbed the sleep crusties from my eyes.

"Now?"

She nodded and tilted her head toward the door.
"Never a better time than now."

"Where are we going?" I whispered back,
afraid to wake Dad
but also wishing
Dad would wake
and chase this secret-keeping feeling away.

Everything is equal parts scary and exciting
in the middle of the night.

"Wherever the road takes us, Tully!"
Mom said,
her words louder,
but her smile dimmer.

She was getting frustrated
with me.

A twinge of worry pinched my ribs.
I was already ruining the adventure.

What I didn't understand until later
is that when Mom says,
"Never a better time than now,"
she means
"There will never *be* another time than now."

I must have paused too long.
The mood inside Mom shifted,
and she stood.

"Never mind, kiddo.
We'll talk about it in the morning," she said,
and closed the door.

When I woke
to the blip-blip, blip-blip, blip-blip of my alarm,
I blinked and thought it had been a dream.

Then I went into the kitchen.
Dad was at the kitchen table,
and Mom was not.

"Where's Mom?"

His eyes
roamed the room
instead of settling on me,
and I knew:
she had gone on her adventure without me.

I looked around the kitchen—
    her favorite blue coffee thermos
    her cucumber lip balm
    her jacket from the swim meet slung over a chair.
She *couldn't* be gone!

Dad handed me a note,
slipped it to me
like you do in class,
like he was afraid to get caught.
He studied his hands on the table
instead of my face as I read
in Mom's scratchy writing:
"Searching for me. XO"

That was it.

That's how my mom says goodbye,
maybe forever.

My chest scrunches now
in this choppy mess of water,
like I can curl up and hide from the worst of it.

Because the worst of it is,
if I had been faster,
been *ready*
like Mom always tells me to be,
I could be there now
with her
wherever she is
on an adventure.

I did not cry.
We are not criers, remember?
And when Dad lifted his hands from the table,
I did not let them fall on my shoulders.
I did not want the weight of a hug
when *I* should have been
GONE.

I ran out the door,
and the sun blinded me.
The fires had moved west in the night,
and the haze had lifted,
and the sky was now a blue so clear
it looked like it went on forever.
I screamed at the blinding sun
and the stupid forever sky.
It wasn't fair
that my worst day
had to be so beautiful.

Nine days later,

when we had begun to live off Chipotle and Thai
because all the organic cheese and yogurt and soy milk
in our fridge had gone bad,
when it was too long to hope Mom was just
"taking the weekend to clear her head,"
I did something I'm not proud of,
but I'm also not *not* proud of it
because it led me to this day, on this lake, in this battle:
I waited until Dad was swallowed up
in the glow of his computer screen,
and I raided Mom's bedside table for clues.
Maybe if I could figure out where she went,
I could run away to join her.

Dad would be fine.
Dad is the lake on a windless summer day—
so calm and clear you can see all the way to the bottom.
Mom is the chop of waves on a yellow-flag day
that you cross your fingers won't turn to red.
Mom needed me.

In the drawer of her side table, I found:
    $1.27 in change
    a couple of Band-Aids
    her favorite bookmark with the Celtic knot
    a pen with the Bank of America logo.
I did not find any clues to where she went.

But I did find the key to get her back:
    a map of the lake with the Godfather swim highlighted

in pink
that we had printed on Dad's printer
and planned one late night over spaghetti
with Dad Googling the youngest person on record
and Mom pointing at me and saying,
"World, meet the next record breaker, right here."
Training was to start in the spring.
Both Mom and Dad would be my support crew
with Dad in charge of navigation
and Mom in charge of snacks/pacing/everything else.
It was going to be epic.
It was going to be an adventure.

I caught the bus to school that day
with the map crinkled in my hand,
then I dragged Arch into the library
and told him my plan.
I'd do it alone—the big swim
in July, just like we planned,
and that would be the key to bringing my family
together again.

I would do it on my own,
and it would be the thing that would
prove to Mom
that she can have her great big adventure
with me
because I am a winner
and I can do HARD THINGS.

And *that's* when Arch swore
to be my support crew,
because my mother had disappeared
and I needed all the support I could get.

At-Risk Youth

End of mile eight.
I can't talk anymore.
I cannot waste breath
on anything but breathing.

I let my mind drift
while my body pushes
longer and harder
than it ever has before.

There is a space
between my first and second toe—
a   gap
big enough that it makes wearing flip-flops impossible.
My dad has it too.

I have one dimple,
just one,
on the right side
so that every time I smile,
it looks like a smirk,
just like my dad.

I have a bump on the bridge of my nose
like I've been in a fight,
but you can't even see it
if you look at me

straight on.
That one's from Mom.

I love cilantro
like her.
Dad says it tastes
like soap.

I eat ice cream cones from the bottom-up
and hot dogs from the middle-out
like her.

My wavy hair
is the same shade of auburn,
and we both have a freckle the size of a kernel of corn
on our shoulders.
Hers is on the left.
Mine is on the right.
When we face each other,
we look like mirror images.

In fifth grade,
the school counselor,
Ms. Jeannie,
brought in a team of nutritionists
to study the school lunch menu
to make sure we were eating a well-balanced diet,
because one of the factors of poor school performance
is a lack of healthy food.

Our school lunches got an A+
with their whole-grain rolls
and green beans
and fruit cups.

We did not tell the team
or Ms. Jeannie
that 90 percent of the time,
we choose chicken wings
and chocolate chip cookies
because Mrs. Tucker
in the kitchen makes them fresh.

Ms. Jeannie was so proud,
her Crocs with socks tapping happy on the linoleum.
She said we were all "on track for success"
with a low percentage of "at-risk" factors.

Arch raised his hand
like I knew he would
and asked,
"At risk for what?"

Ms. Jeannie crossed her arms over her Patagonia fleece
and said, like it was obvious,
"At risk for not transitioning into productive adults."

We stared at her forehead
until the silence grew so uncomfortable
she filled it with words to explain her explanation.

"We are all working hard
to help you do well in school
and improve your math and science and . . . and art!"
she said to Arch.
"But there are other factors"—
she fiddled with the zipper on her jacket—
"that can affect your success."

"Like what?" Arch asked
because he cared,
but also because he didn't want
to go back
to math.

"Like nutrition,"
Ms. Jeannie said,
holding up her fingers and ticking things off.
"And family income levels
and crime rates in the community
and access to after-school programs
and—"

"Does that mean you're going to let us
start a street hockey team?"
Melissa Reyes shouted from the back,
which took the conversation off the rails
as more kids shouted which things
they wanted to do for free
after school
until Principal Blackburn

stepped in
and shooed everybody
back to class.

I wouldn't say this to Ms. Jeannie
because I am not brave like Arch,
but "at-risk" is a dumb term
if you ask me.

Flood.
Car crash.
Wildfire.
Earthquake.
Sinkhole.
Sickness.
Sadness.
Everybody's *at risk* of something.

Now I'm thinking about the cut on my thumb.
I feel around the edges
for the invisible bacteria
I'm sure have started to spread.

I kick harder than I should
and give my arms a break
even though I know
I need to use my upper body
to pull
instead of my legs
to push.

Anil, the therapist
Dad makes me see
since Mom disappeared,
talks a lot about how depression
can be an invisible disease
and how you can't always tell
what's going on with a person
when you look at the outside.

I have her nose.
Her hair.
Her freckle.

I shiver in the water
as a cloud passes over.

And like the cloud
dragged it here
comes a thought. . . .
Am I "at risk" for her depression too?

Overhead, the sky rumbles.
The storm we thought we'd dodged
is blowing back in.

HOUR FIVE

Rules Are Made to Be Broken

"Distance remaining: 3.75 miles.

Time elapsed: five hours and three minutes.

Chance of rain: 78 percent,"

Arch narrates into the camera.

The cloud that followed me into mile six

has brought friends—

    a trail of dark shapes in the sky

    that shifts into

        crooked dragons

        clawed dinosaurs

        cruel-mouthed sea monsters.

My breath hitches.

A dragon would be better than a storm.

Anything would be better than a storm.

I would fight Tessie,

the legendary monster of Lake Tahoe,

if it would keep the thunder and lightning away.

Because the number one rule of open-water swimming is:

when you hear thunder, clear the water.

I snuck out,

trained in secret,

forged my mom's signature on the safety waiver,

and lied to my dad for the last five hours about where I am.

But I cannot mess around with a storm. . . .

Can I?

At the Sequoia Club,
a regulation hangs
above the door to the fitness center.
It is printed in black letters
on a white sign
and framed in gold
so no one can miss it.
It reads:
"NO CHILDREN UNDER TWELVE
WITHOUT ADULT SUPERVISION."

I spent every afternoon at Sequoia
from the moment I could swim.
I knew that the corner
    by the vending machine
    outside the women's locker room
    was the best place to cool off after practice
    because that's where the air-conditioning blew hardest.
I knew that Donna
    at the concession stand
    by the pool
    would give me a free Cola ICEE
    on Wednesdays.
I knew that the empty yoga studio
    when the floors had been waxed
    and the mats had been rolled

after the instructors had gone home
was the best place to squeak my tennis shoes.
And I knew *never* to go in the fitness center
with the elliptical machines
and treadmills
and free weights
without Mom.

But one Friday afternoon when I was seven,
Mom had to cancel swim practice.
The chemicals in the indoor pool
needed adjusting
or something.

So she gave me a dollar for the vending machine,
told me to stay outdoors or in her office,
and sent me "to play."
I crumpled the money in my fist
and stomped away.

I'd thought we could hang
together for once
without it having to be about swim.
But I guess she had PT clients to see
who were more important than me.

Two Reese's Cups later and I was bored
and angry.
So I did the one thing I could think of

that would make Mom
angry too.

I snuck into the fitness center,
hopped on a treadmill
that faced away
from the wall of mirrors,
and hit start.

I smiled over my shoulder
at the sight of me
jogging with a chocolate-covered grin.

The man running on my left
didn't even notice.
He was absorbed in the stats
on the tiny screen
that measure your distance/pace/calories.

I got enough
distance/pace/calories talk
from Mom,
so I switched it to TV mode.

Have you ever tried
to change a channel
and lower the volume
while moving your feet
at   the   same   pace

on a moving walkway?

I could do hard things.
But I could not do that.

I slipped,
then tripped
on my own foot
and fell to my knees.

I shot back like a rocket
into the wall of mirrors.

I heard the cr-aaaack before I saw it or felt it.
Then I heard it again
as I pulled my knee out of the glass.
The crack crawled across the wall,
a web spun
by an invisible spider
I wished would swallow me
whole.

The treadmills stopped.
The ellipticals stopped.
The weight lifting stopped.

Like a mass of aliens
sensing an invader,
all the adults
turned

as one

to me.

I had never seen Theo, the manager, run until that day.

His red polo shirt came untucked

from his chinos

as he scooped me up

and out of sight

while the cut on my leg

dripped too-bright blood

down

the

hall,

all

over

the

carpet.

It should have stung,

but I was more afraid

of Mom

than the

cut.

She met me in the clinic,

where she waved away the nurse,

who had been wincing every time

she picked a piece of glass from my knee.

Mom was less gentle.

She squatted in front of my plastic chair.
My heart beat
with   a   steady   and   terrified   thump.

When she dowsed my knee with peroxide,
I didn't flinch.
I knew better.

But then . . .
she leaned over,
the tip of her ponytail flicking my shin like a paintbrush,
and softly blew on the crisscross cuts
with her warm breath.

I started to cry.

"I broke the wall!"
I wailed,
because it was easier to say than
I broke myself
and my promise to you.

She didn't say a word
as she wound gauze and tape
over the wound,
which made me cry harder.
I wanted her to tell me
everything would be okay.
I wanted her to blow on it again,
hug me,

hold my hand.

Instead, she took my face in both her hands
and leaned in close
so I caught the smell of cucumber lip balm.
"Did you see how I wrapped it?" she asked.
I nodded.
"Could you do it again if you had to?"
I nodded.
"Good," she said, and touched the tip of my nose.
I risked a smile.
"Because I'm not always going to be here
to pick up the pieces."

The first drops of cold rain
bring me back to the present,
prickling my cheek as I turn for a breath.

I am hoping it's too small a drizzle
for Arch to notice
when a boom of thunder
shuts that train of thought
right down.

On my left,
Arch slumps in his seat.
"Do you want to call it, or me?"

I wait,
watch for the flash,

then shake my head
and hold up eight fingers
because I am too tired to talk.

Eight seconds between
lightning
and
thunder.

If Mom taught me one thing,
it's how to take care of myself.

The storm is still miles away,
and I am too close to quit.

Zing

It is not eight seconds. It is six when
a flash turns the far mountains black
against a sky the color of rotten plums.
Tiny hairs on my arm rise to greet the
electricity like a friend. But it is not a
friend. It is a lasso waiting to snag me
then zap me and roast me, because the
first thing you learn on the beach from
the lifeguards with their whistles and
warning flags is this: water in a storm is not your friend.
It's a pan ready to fry as that stream of hot current hits,
and then it spreads all that electricity just like butter
oozing into the lake, sizzling everything it touches.

A zigzag of light streaks across the sky like veins
in a tree and the veins in my arm. My heart trips
over itself in a hurry to hide. I shut my eyes, but
the flash stays bright, and I'm six again, tucking
my head into Mom's neck while she dances
with me in her arms in the first spring rain.
"For luck," she says, and laughs when a
zing of lighting shatters the purple sky.
"Too dangerous," Dad says, and shoos
us in, and I am glad even though she
complains he chased away the luck.
Right now the air fizzes and my
ears buzz. But I can't stop.
Because if I run from
danger, then luck
might run
from
me.

Stuck in the Fishbowl

"Tully, we have to call it,"
Arch yells
at me,
not *to* me
from the kayak,
where he sits with the phone in his hand.

It's blowing up
with calls
and texts
and voicemails—
so many notifications for the obvious:
the parents know what's up.

I shake my head
and turn away from him,
my body fighting a wind
that reminds me of the waves
I beat back in the San Francisco Bay.
I did it before.
I can do it again.

"They know we're on the water!
They tracked my phone,"
Arch says,
holding it up
as if I need

proof.
As if anything
would make me stop.

"Put that thing away
or the rain'll ruin it!"
I shout with an extra puff of breath
I do not have.
What a selfless thing,
to spend precious energy
so his phone stays safe,
right?
(And save our footage and silence the parental alerts.)

They were going to catch on eventually.
But they don't know *where*
on the lake
I am.

A wave slaps me in the face
when I come up for air,
and I choke.
How am I supposed to breathe when
    above

         and

            under
water are starting to feel the same?

I have to be careful now.
I cannot afford to swallow the lake

I am supposed to be
swimming through.

The current drags me backward,
every stroke
a slip down the mountain,
scrabbling at weeds.

The harder I dig,
the tighter the tide pulls against me.
I am a yo-yo
that has reached
the length of its
S
T
R
I
N
G.

Mom's voice in my head,
laughing,
saying the thing she's always said
when a hike/run/swim gets hard:
It keeps things interesting. It proves you're alive.

*An easy life is a boring life,
and boredom is a kind of death,*
she said.

I catch another waveintheface

and cough up more water.

A blast of lightning turns the lake molten silver,
and I have just enough time to think,
Death is also a kind of death.
I don't want to die out here
before thunder rattles my eardrums.

I dive deep to escape the noise,
a fish with nowhere else to go.

The first time I had to see Anil, the therapist,
he showed me a picture of a fish in a bowl.

"Tully," he said, and then he said "Tully" again
because he liked to use the same trick
that teachers use
when they think you are not
paying attention:
play your name on repeat.

I made eye contact
so he would stop.

"Did you know, Tully"—one more for good measure—
"that fish get depressed?"
He asked it in a way
that told me he hoped I didn't,
because he wanted to explain it to me.

I shook my head.

I had still not decided if I was going to speak to him
or not.
He sat in a chair across from me instead of behind a desk,
which I liked,
but he was also here to make me talk about my feelings,
which I did not like.

He handed me a picture
of a clear bowl of water
with one single striped fish
hovering in the middle.

"It's true,"
he said, and then paused to wipe down
his frameless glasses
to build anticipation, I guess,
or maybe there really was a smudge.
"When researchers studied a group of zebra fish,
they noticed that some of them,
the ones who were depressed,
tended to float lower in the water
than their counterparts."

Sink or swim, I heard Mom say in my head
before I could shake it away.

In an experiment of my own,
I decided to make a face
halfway between
interested

and
sleepy
and let Anil decide what to do with it.

He decided to keep talking.
"We don't know what caused the fish to be depressed,
but we do know
that when they were given
a small dose of antidepressants,
the fish floated to the top!"

Smile lines crinkled the corners of his brown eyes.
Did he expect applause?
I made my sleepy face.

He continued.
"The medicine wasn't a magical cure.
As I am sure you know.
But it served as a reminder
to the fish
to look up."

He smiled.
I did not.

I knew what he was trying to do.
He wanted me to know that my mother leaving
was not my fault.
She had stopped taking her medication.
She had stopped seeing her own therapist.

She made a series of choices
that caused her depression to get worse until
like
dominoes
lined
up
in
a
row,
our whole lives toppled to the ground.

But I knew the truth.
It wasn't the lack of medicine
or lack of therapy
or lack of rest.
It was the lack of *adventure*.

My mother has always needed a challenge.
And somehow,
along the way,
her life here
on the lake
with me and Dad
had gotten too small,
so she jumped the bowl
and left me
floating in the middle.

But I'm stirring things up again
so she'll have a reason

to come back.
Except . . .
Why couldn't she just wait?
A few more hours?
A few more days?
A few more months until summer
and we could be doing this together
right now?
Why does it always have to be her way
or not at all?
Why didn't she love me enough
to wait?

I break the surface
and gasp.

No!
A thought like that will drag me down
quicker than any storm.

She loves me.
She *does*.

I just have to hang on a little bit longer.

There's a First Time for Everything

Arch is not talking to me.
Or if he is,
I can't hear him
over the wind and the rain.

My swim cap
has come loose
on one side,
and hair spills out
in a tangle
that clings to my face
and wraps around my goggles
if I turn my head the wrong way.

I can't stop thinking about what Anil said
about the zebra fish
and wishing I hadn't told him what I did
in our next session.

He tricked me
with those clear brown eyes
that didn't dart away
or judge
behind his clean glasses.

Our family has things
we are not supposed to talk about,

that sit in the corner of the room
like a pile of dirty clothes
which has been there so long
you stop seeing it.

The thing I never even told Arch
but somehow let slip to Anil
was that this was not the only time Mom left.

I was five
when she disappeared the first time.
It was three days before Christmas.

Mom went out to buy wrapping paper
to cover the jacket
we bought for "Jaqueline, Age 5"—
a name we plucked off the Angel Tree
at the Salvation Army.

Because I didn't know how
Angel Trees worked,
I was excited about Jaqueline.
I thought we would become friends.

I was also so jealous of her new jacket,
the puffer with the violet butterflies,
that when we picked it out
I whined to Mom and Dad
that I wanted it for myself.
Mom ignored me.

But Dad grinned and touched his fingertip
to my dimple that matches his,
his way of saying,
I hear you, kiddo,
without actually having to say yes or no.

I didn't understand that
I would never meet "Jaqueline, Age 5,"
who would get our gifts
on Christmas Day
when she came to the Salvation Army
for lunch.

I didn't understand a lot of things.

That night,
when Mom did not return with the wrapping paper
or dinner,
Dad fixed me chicken noodle soup
from a can
and put me to bed
with a kiss
and a list
of things I wanted to do tomorrow
on Christmas Eve.

When I woke,
I pressed my nose to the burning-cold glass of my window
to view the new snow that had fallen overnight.
It covered the driveway

where Mom's car should have been—
a smooth, white sheet
pulled tight.

Dad and I played Monopoly.
He let me cheat.
We drank not-hot-enough hot chocolate
with not-small-enough marshmallows.

We watched *Elf*
and *Rudolph*
and *The Grinch*,
and still
Mom did not come home,
and still
Dad did not talk about it.

I didn't ask.

Parents were weird.
They did strange things all the time
like floss with those floss sticks
and drink black coffee
and complain about running out of coffee
after they said they needed to cut back.

I told myself that if Dad wasn't worried,
I shouldn't be either,
even though my stomach was squirmy all day.

That night,
I wrapped Jaqueline's present
in the scraps of tissue and bits of wrapping paper
we had left over from last year.
Dad clapped his hands
and called it a masterpiece.
I was five,
but I wasn't a fool.
It looked like a papier-mâché blob.

We set it under the Christmas tree anyway,
where Santa would leave
all my presents
if I had been
good.

That night I fell asleep
wondering if *Santa* was good.
Why would he make me
brush my teeth for two full minutes,
wash my hair when it wasn't dirty,
give Jaqueline a present wrapped in scraps,
and keep my mom away on the most important night
of the year
if he was good?

When I got up on Christmas Day,
I did not look out the window.
I was scared to see
what wasn't there.

But then Mom burst into my room
holding my snow pants and a violet puffer jacket
just like Jaqueline's.
"Suit up, T,
because *we* are going sledding!"
she sang,
and just like that,
the squirmy feeling from the last two days
was gone.

I hopped into the hall,
one leg half-in
and half-out
of my pants,
to spy a row of presents under the tree
for me.
Jaqueline's gift
was there too,
rewrapped
so that it glittered with silver snowflakes.
My blob was gone.

I ran to Dad first
and buried my face
in his blue nubby sweatshirt,
right next to his neck,
where his beard
had started to grow in.

I was still scared

to look too hard at Mom
in case she disappeared.

She sat down next to me
on the couch in front of the tree.
I snuck a glance at her as she helped me lace my boots.

Her hair was shorter,
chopped to her shoulders
instead of falling all the way down her back in waves.
She smelled different too,
waxy soap and morning breath.

When she looked at me,
dark half-moon shadows
hung under her eyes
like she hadn't slept
in all the time she had been gone
and whatever had kept her up
was worse than the worst scary story
I could ever imagine.

The squirmy feeling in my stomach
came back.

But then Dad tickled me,
and Mom laughed,
and we all got up
to stomp
        to the back deck
                to grab the sleds.

The moment passed.

Santa had left presents.
Mom came back.
Jaqueline got a nicely wrapped gift.
I must have been good enough
after all.
So I pushed the squirmy feeling
to the way, way, waaaaaayyyy
back of my mind
like I knew they wanted me to.

Until I told Anil . . .

When I finished the story of Mom's Christmas
disappearance,
he started to offer me a tissue, then stopped,
which I appreciated because I wasn't crying.
I *wasn't*.
Instead, he said
in a voice warm as a towel from the dryer,
"I'm sorry your mother did that to you."

I sat up straighter.
"Did what to me?
My mom didn't *do* anything to me."

"She left," he said, so quietly I almost leaned forward
before I remembered I didn't care what he said.

His logic stung

like a sweat bee—
a tiny pinprick of betrayal after everything I told him.
He was supposed to be on our side. Me *and* Mom's.

"But that, that's—" I sputtered.
"You don't understand!"

"Help me understand."

"We were out of wrapping paper.
Christmas is always a hard time of year!
I was complaining about not getting the jacket.
I—I didn't leave with her when she asked . . . ," I choke out.

Now I was getting confused,
flip-flopping Mom's disappearances.

"Tully," he said,
not to get my attention,
but because he could tell I was getting riled up,
"depression is a chemical imbalance—"

I opened my mouth.
He touched a hand to his chest.
He was not done.

"You," Anil said in his softest voice yet,
"did not cause your mother's depression,
and you are not responsible for fixing it."

"I *know*," I said,
and then didn't say anything else the rest of the session
or the one after that
or the one after that,
because he can't make me talk.

Except now . . .
everything's spilling out
of my mind
with every mile,
and I'm scared
it's something I can't outpace.

Lightning Never Strikes the Same Place Twice

The storm breaks the sky open
like a cracked egg
oozing electricity.

I feel it in my chest
before another lightning strike
lights up the sky
even closer this time.

It can't be over yet.
It can't.

I never told Dad that Mom asked me to leave with her
that night.

I never told Mom that Dad took me to IHOP
when she didn't come home for dinner.

I never told Dad that Mom snuck out for bike rides
when she was supposed to rest.

I never told Mom that Dad made better spaghetti
than her.

I never told Dad that Mom would play his Nintendo
when she couldn't sit still.

I never told Mom that Dad knew she played his Nintendo,
which is why he always left it set to her favorite game.

I never told Dad that I use Mom's lip balm
so I can smell like her.

I never told Mom that I missed her sometimes,
even when she was there.

I never told Dad that Mom would order her therapist
not to talk to Dad.

I never told Mom that Dad tried to talk to her therapist
anyway.

I never told Dad that I'm glad
he's here.

I never told Mom that I'm mad
she's gone.

I never told Dad why I need to do this swim
with or without him.

I never told Mom that I could do this swim
with or without her.

And now I'm running out of time.

Miracles

If I could talk to her right now,
in the middle of the lake
in the middle of a storm,
this is what I'd say:

Maybe if I pretend you are dead, it would be easier.

Because if you are dead,
then I can be sad
and it won't be my fault
that you're gone.

If you are dead,
it could be from cancer
or some really rare disease
that would prove
you did not leave because of
who I am
or am not.

People would feel sorry for me—
not in the awkward way they do now,
whispering to their neighbors
in the grocery store/school hall/therapist's waiting room—
but in a good way
that makes them offer casseroles and cookies and hand-me-

D
O
W
N
S.

They would bring foil-wrapped dishes
and Trader Joe's snacks
and put a warm hand on my shoulder and say,
"She's in a better place"
and
"She's at peace now,"
which is a load of crap,
but it beats
all the rumors
circling
behind my back.

If you are dead,
then I can be one-half an orphan,
which is better
than one-half abandoned,
which is not my fault
according to Anil,
but what does he know?

If you are dead,
I can miss you more
and hate you less.

If you are dead,
you coming back
when I finish this swim
could be
a miracle.

Undivided Attention

Arch is waving
an emergency flare
in the air
and threatening to set it off
if I don't stop.

I shout, "No!"
which he can't hear
over the
crashingwaves
roaringwind
slashingrain.

I burrow into the pain in my chest
that Mom always told me
was the body's turning point,
when the mind switches off
and you become a machine
of efficiency.

But my mind isn't turning off.

One time during speech class,
our teacher brought in
a motivational speaker.

He wore a sun visor inside
and ran his own
wellness center
in Reno.

He passed out
personal mantras on cards
and walked up and down the aisles,
looking at every student
in turn
as he told us
his life story
of rags to riches.
How he went from selling protein powder
at GNC
to starting his own business
on IG.

He became an influencer
of people's
minds
instead of
their bodies, he said.

I tuned him out
and looked at my mint-green mantra card,
which read,
"I am enough."

People paid for this?

To have him tell them
they are fine
just as they are?

Mom would disagree.
She says
people are always in a state of becoming.
Whether it's
less
or
more
is up to them.

I squeeze my eyes shut tight
against another flash of lightning,
a black line reflected on my eyelids,
the sky's colors
in reverse.

The self-improvement guru
did teach me one trick
that I never told Mom
or Dad
or Anil.

Staring down the class, he said,
"You can never underestimate the importance of
Eye Contact."

"The eyes are the windows to the soul,"

he said.
"Liars always look up and to the left,"
he said.
"Pupils dilate with fear,"
he said.
"Rapid blinking signals panic,"
he said.
"And most importantly"—
he glared at each and every one of us—
"you can't trust a person
who won't meet your gaze."

I didn't need to see
Mom quit her meds
or stop sleeping
or start training for another triathlon
to know a Blue Period
when I saw one.

It was in her eyes.

It came in a wave
that started as a ripple,
that rose to a swell,
that turned into a tsunami,
that all began with one thing:
lack of eye contact.

We would be eating dinner,
her at the counter and

Dad and me at the table.
But instead of glancing up
at Dad's terrible *Game of Thrones* jokes
and my equally terrible TikTok recaps,
she would smile
with her eyes
on her phone.

When she woke me up
in the morning
with a kiss on my forehead
after her run,
she was already pulling away
before I could see her face.

When she yelled through cupped hands at practice
for me to *dig deeper! go faster!*,
she would watch the clock,
and in her face
was an absence.

You don't have to tell me
the importance of eye contact.
I lived it every day.

The guru's card was wrong—

I am not enough.

HOUR SIX

BOOM

BOOM

Thunder shakes the air
like a drum.

I dive deep under the water, where it is quiet,
while Arch
not-so-quietly
yells at me
through the bullhorn.

"TULLY BIRCH, GET OUT OF THE WATER NOW!"

He sounds like his mom,
who is not a yeller,
so when she does yell
it comes out rusty
and wavering
but impossible to ignore.

I dive deeper
until the balloon in my chest
is shriveled
to nothing
and
I
cannot

last
another
beat
before
surfacing.

I am met with screaming wind
whooshing waves
roaring thunder
hissing lightning
spitting rain.
But from my best friend?
Silence.

I breathe
and turn to my left.
No Arch.

I breathe again
and turn right.
No Arch.

Then I look straight ahead
to see my friend
who swore to support me
no matter what
parked in my path
with his oar held high
like Gandalf's staff,
ready to

STOP me.

I swerve and he back paddles
to stay in front,
an awkward middle school dance
acted out on water.

"Get out of my way, Arch!"
I croak with all the voice I have left.

"No!" he shouts,
his cheeks red with anger and fear
and his jacket plastered to his chest.

I scream in my head
because I don't have the energy
to scream out loud.

Diving under again,
I surface
beyond him.
Out of sight,
out of mind,
right?

"Tully, wait, I—!" he cries,
but the wind
bats his words away.

I concentrate on my strokes,

stretching out
so I am longer and stronger than I have ever been,
a sleek arrow in the water,
pointed straight for shore.

BOOM
BOOM
BOOM

The air crackles and fizzes
around me.

I time my strokes to the rhythm of the storm.

Good Night

After Mom left,
time seemed to stop.
March stayed cold,
the edges of the lake rimmed in ice
like an overgrown nail.

I felt it in my bones.
My blood thickandslushy
like the water.

I could not eat.
I could not sleep.
I could not swim.

When I was little,
Dad was in charge of bedtime.
He helped brush my hair,
which I hated.
He helped brush my teeth,
which I hated.
But then he helped pick out a story,
which I loved.

He walked me over
            to the pile of books
                    that never quite made it
                        back onto the bookshelf,

and we took our time selecting the perfect
ones.

He made sure I had water next to the bed,
and he pulled the covers up to my chin,
and then he read
    Pete the Cat
    Pinkalicious
    I Am Courage
    I Am Love
    I Am Human
because it was never just *one* book
or one glass of water
or one trip to the bathroom
or one "good night, I love you."

It went on and on,
and Dad never checked his watch
(he couldn't if he wanted to
because I broke the strap
using it as an ankle bracelet).
His oldest and worst joke whenever we are late is still:
"Tully! You made me lose track of time!"

Bedtime would never stop
if I had any say in it,
which I did not,
because every night
Mom's shadow would fall across the hall,
and she would

rap, rap, rap
her knuckles on the doorframe and say,
"That's it. Both of you."

She would say it with a smile,
but it was a smile you did not argue with.

Dad would get up off my floor with a grunt
and kiss me one more time
and walk to Mom,
and that was it.
Good night, Tully.

Dad was great for entertainment
But Mom was THE MOM.
                        THE DISCIPLINER.
                        THE ORGANIZER.
                        THE BONES of our little family so we did not
                        turn to mush.

With no Mom to order me to sleep after she left,
I stopped.

I was a Tully zombie
shuffling the halls of school,
going through the motions
but not living.

I don't know how he knew.
It's not like we did bedtime anymore.

But sometime in late March,
Dad figured it out.

He started showing up again,
    outside my room,
    on the ground,
    with his back against the wall
    and laptop open.
He sat for hours.

While the hallway clock ticked,
I counted the keys he clicked
like some people count sheep.

Tick-tock
click-clack
tick-click
tock-clack . . .
Eventually, I slept.

When March turned to April,
the lake began to thaw
and my mind began to work again
toward the goal
of the Godfather swim.

I had a mission to pull Mom back.
I closed my door.
I didn't need Dad anymore.

As my arms churn against waves
that feel less like they are carrying me
and more like they are holding me down,
I wonder now
how long he lasted.

How many days/weeks/months did he sit there
before finally calling it a night?

Maybe tonight
he will be there again,
click-clack,
tap-tapping away
so I won't be alone
after this is done.

When I remember to breathe in,
it burns.

Dropping

A

drop of

rain an hour ago

is how it started. Just

a plink on the lake in front of

me that was so quick to disappear

I thought I imagined it. Then it prickled

my arms like the softest tap on my shoulder

by a friend ready to whisper a secret. But the rain

is not my friend. Now it is a plague—a swarm of bees,

a murder of crows, a nest of mosquitoes here to bury me

with sheer volume. You can drown in half an inch of rainwater,

they say. And yet . . . I tilt my head up to the sky and let it prick my face,

like the tines of a fork. Time to wake up, Tully. Get moving. When you're stuck,

some people call that treading water. Enough of that. *If you are not moving forward,*

you are falling back. That is what Mom always said. Mom. Mom once raced in a storm.

ost her footing on loose gravel. Cut her knee open on a rock. Still finished third with blood

ipping into her sock. And here I am worried about a little rain. And a cut on my finger that

n't really need a Band-Aid if I'm being honest. I dive deeper, where the wind and the rain

n't touch me. Somewhere down here there has to be a quiet space that is safe from all the

oise. Mom loves noise. She loves cheers from the fans and the echoing slaps of hands on

he edge of the pool, and most of all, she loves the applause at the end. Maybe I was too

quiet. That was why she had to go. There wasn't enough applause. I should come up

for air soon. Arch will be wondering where I am. But I'm so tired. And it's so quiet,

and the final mile is harder than the last eleven put together. I don't know why

I thought I could do this. I am not Mom. I am not tough. I don't like the noise.

I like the calm down here where nobody needs anything from me and I

can just be me. But who am I without something to push for?

My lungs are burning more than my arms. The balloon

inside is almost empty. I have a choice to make:

I can stay down here, or I can

rise and fight.

The Breaking Point

"Tully!"
Arch yells
from behind me.

"TULLYTULLYTULLY!"

The waves along the surface
stir me like soup,
making it hard to keep my head under
and hide.

Arch paddles closer.
My lungs
    burn
    beg
    beat
against their cage.

"TULLY BIRCH, GET YOUR STUPID HEAD
OUT OF THE STUPID WATER.
I ALREADY CALLED YOUR DAD!"

My head lifts
all on its own.
I take a great, heaving breath that
brings my chest right out of the water.

"You didn't!" I scream.

He winces,

his hair a flat cap on his forehead.

I don't think he heard the actual words

over the storm,

but he got the general idea.

I swim closer,

close enough to his bright blue kayak

that I could touch it

if I wanted to,

which I don't,

because that would mean

a disqualification,

and I am

NOT QUITTING

yet.

I lean closer

and lift my goggles

from my swollen face.

"How could you?"

I rasp.

"Water patrol is on its way," he says,

which isn't an answer.

Red blooms across his cheeks—

embarrassment/anger/fear—

me + the storm = Arch's worst nightmare.

The paddle hangs limp in his hands,
which are wrinkled from water
and twisting with worry
while we blow about in the wind.

Under the rain
lashing his face,
I notice something else:
Arch is crying.

My stomach cramps
with pain
that is not
from hunger.

Everybody has a breaking point.
This is mine.

Alone

I did this.
I put my best friend in danger.
I am dragging him down with me
just like I dragged down Mom.
It's why she had to leave.
And it's not fair to Arch.

Behind him, lightning streaks
across the sky,
too close.
The hairs on both our arms
rise.

Arch drops his phone.
It hits the edge of the kayak
and tumbles into the water.
I flinch.
My only proof that I did this thing is
sinking
to the bottom of the lake.

"Tully, I'm sorry!
I can't do this by myself!
I thought I could be your support crew.
But if something happens,
I can't save you!"
It is not a shout or a yell or a scream.

It is a whisper, because we
are close enough to read lips,
to see into each other's eyes.
I look away first.

He needs to
go home,
get dry,
eat a bowl of cereal,
make some art.

But I can't stop,
even if there's no one to see.

I dive again
but not before
waving goodbye.

I can give him that.

He doesn't understand the choice I just made
until I am out of reach.
I see it in his face
when he realizes his friend
has left him.

A flash of lightning freeze-frames the moment.

It's better this way.
He'll be better this way.

Mom has been training me for this my whole life.
Swimming might be a team sport,
but everyone knows
once you're in the water,
you are
alone.

A Body in Motion

I am still feet from Arch, but we are already worlds apart. It was easier to say goodbye than I thought it would be. Maybe this is how Mom did it. Quick like a paper cut. I can see the shore now, a murky gray line in the distance bordered by round, white rocks that look like gumballs spilled from a machine. I am so close. But I can hear the rattle of an engine behind, over the sound of the thunder that rocks me back and forth in the water like a bottle cap. Someone's coming.

I am a body in motion. I am a body. In motion. I am a body in a body of water. We are two bodies together with the same goal: to reach the shore. You do not have to tell your heart to beat or your lungs to breathe or your eyes to blink. At this point in the swim, I do not have to tell my legs to kick, my arms to reach, my head to turn. I am a body in motion that is now a machine. Please, whoever you are, just let me go until I run myself ashore. Please.

Fishing is the only outdoor sport Dad likes to do. Probably because it involves sitting for long periods of time. And listening to birds/crickets/Van Morrison. He tried to take me a few times. But I couldn't sit still. I would love to be still. Now. But my body is a body in motion. In a body of water. And we are two bodies that cannot be stopped until we reach the shore.

Water-Daughter

"Tully! Stop!" Dad yells.

Dad. He found me.
In the middle of the lake,
in a white swim cap,
surrounded by white-capped waves.
He came.

For one millionth of a second,
a thought splits me in two—
I could go to him.

I could raise my arm high in the air,
and he would lift me out
of this mess.

He looks like a real sailor
with a black beanie on his head
and a bright yellow rain jacket unzipped
and flying in the wind
that he is creating
from slicing through the water
to get to me.

Wait . . .
the wind
he is creating.
I pause to look up.

Is it brighter?
The gray seems less gray,
a wisp of blue pushing through.

And the lightning . . .
I scan the horizon.
Nothing.
The lightning has stopped,
packed it in, and called it a day,
went home holding thunder's hand.

The rain still crashes down.
Pellets hit the waves like bullets,
but they are falling straight down
instead of sideways.
I am on the outer edge
of the storm.

I *can't* quit now.

Dad crisscrosses his hands over his head
like the reason I am not swimming toward him
is simply because I have not spotted
his rusted metal boat.

He can't get any closer to me
without cutting the engine
or risk
cutting me
on the engine.
He needs me to come to him.

If I keep moving,
he has no choice
but to stay back.

Arch hovers behind him
in his kayak,
paddle in lap,
head hung low.
Now that we've moved from red-flag
to yellow-flag weather,
he won't look at me.

I want to tell him
not to be mad at himself that he called Dad.
This is not his fault.
None of this is his fault,
like Anil told me.
But like me,
he probably wouldn't believe it.

And anyway, I think,
and slink farther away.

I have already cut
too many cords
to that life raft.
I can't go back.
And I am so close,
soclosesoclosesoclose.

Even the rain is slowing now.

Less, lesser, least,
until it is gone
and I have a clear view of the shore.

Seagulls fight over
limp bits of pondweed
washed up
on the sand
from the storm.

But the water is still a weight
dragging me down
instead of lifting me up
like it promised.

Mom promised
to train me for this.
Mom promised
to take her pills.
Mom promised
to take it easy.
Mom promised
to love
me.

Swimming is who I am.
It's WHAT I am.
I am sun-bleached hair,
goggle-creased cheeks,
cracked lips,
freckled shoulders,

prune-y fingertips.
I *am* the water.

Without it, I am nothing.
Without it, I am a girl missing her mom,
who couldn't care less about her water-daughter.

The sun winks overhead
as the last of the clouds
evaporates
into
  mist.

I bob
in place
like a buoy.
The shore is no closer.
A mirage that fades
in   and   out.

What's the point
of breaking this record?

What's the point
of loving someone
if you can't be sure
they'll love you back?

Anil was right.
I can't fix Mom.

So what's the point?

I flip over on my back
and let my headsinkbackarmsfloatouttoespointup
until I can't see the lake,
only sky.

It looks just like the water—
the same turquoise,
wispy clouds like foamy waves.

Without the water, I am nothing.
Without her, I am nothing.
The water-daughter.

I turn facedown
and stop the motions—
the useless arm-over-arm
the worthless scissor kicks
the hopeless head turns
that have gotten me so far
                    but not far enough.

It feels good
to
fall.

My Father's Daughter

When the hand grips me,
it is not kind.

It is a yank
and a pull,
and then I am on my back
with my head
against a shoulder
that shakes.

Or maybe that's me
shaking/coughing/spitting
and clawing
at the hand that holds me up.

The boat drifts behind us,
sharp gasoline tang in the air,
motor idling impatiently
while Arch
looks everywhere
but at me.

Just beyond him,
a cruiser from the water patrol
waits and watches.

"No!" I scream,

but there is no sound.

I try again.

"Dad, no!"
The words scrape their nails along my throat.

"Please," I whisper into his shirt.

"Tully, my girl,"
Dad says,
hugging me so tight it hurts.
"I won't let you go."

Our breaths fog his glasses.
His arms slide an inch down my shoulders
as he shifts to keep us steady.

I lay my head back against his chest
to rest
for just a minute.
He makes a sobbing sound,
once,
before his scratchy chin
brushes my forehead.

"My girl, my girl, my girl,"
he chokes out over and over again.

"Please, Dad,

the storm's over,"
I say,
but I'm not sure which one I mean—
the one out here
or the one inside me.

Together we look at the blue, blue sky.

All I know is,
with Dad's arms around me
and Arch nearby,
I don't want to sink anymore.
I want to *finish*.

"I'm almost there.
Let me go."
I beg him with my eyes
because it hurts to find more words.

"I'm not leaving you,"
he says like a threat.

"Then come with me,"
I say like a plea.

A ripple of water sends us bobbing again.
Arch has climbed into the boat
and is lashing his kayak to the side.
He's telling Dad to do it.
He'll get the boat.

Even after I abandoned him,
Arch is still helping me out.

Dad shakes his head
but releases me
in the same motion.
For a second, I drop
until my body remembers
it still has a job to do.

He waves to the coast guard,
a signal to return to shore,
that we are okay
or will be.

Dad dog-paddles next to me
in his tennis shoes and denim jeans
on his first open-water swim
as I force my arms to find a rhythm.

I never told Dad that Mom asked me to go with her.
But I told Anil.

Anil said, not unkindly,
"You don't ask a person
that kind of question
and not wait for an answer
unless you already know what you want."

Mom walked away

and Dad jumped in to save me,
because Dad doesn't give up.

I am my father's daughter.

How It Ends

Air temp: 75 degrees.
Water temp: 70 degrees.
Body temp: 98.0 degrees.
Mental state of swimmer: Done.
Mental state of support crew: Done and done.

The sand crumbles between my fingers
when I crawl out of the water
on my hands and knees.
It should feel like a victory,
but all I want to do is sleep.

"Time!" Arch shouts
from somewhere behind.
"Six hours and seven minutes!"

I lie flat on the shore
with the pondweed,
like another thing washed up
by the storm.

When I lift my goggles,
they make a suction-cup squelch.
I throw them to the side
to rub the deep ridges
on my forehead
and cheeks.

My teeth ache
like they used to
when I got my braces tightened.

I am finally still,
but the land seems to move
under my body.
I fight the urge to vomit.

"Up, *now*,"
Dad orders,
and tugs at my hands
until I am sitting
and he can drape a towel
over my aching shoulders.
It smells of lavender detergent,
of home,
of Mom.

My heart flutters
like a leaf in the wind
before it steadies
into a slow
and weary beat.

"You did it!"
Arch whoops,
frightening the sandpipers
marching by in a line
as he stumbles from the boat

edging the shore.

"You are the youngest person in history
to make the Godfather swim!"
His shadow over my legs
makes me shiver.
He grins down at me
and does not say,
You are a bad friend
and
I will never speak to you again,
because Arch really is
a hero.

I swallow my sorrys
to save for later when he's willing to hear them
and say instead,
"We didn't even get it on film.
And I broke the rules."

Arch holds the bell out.
"Ring it."

I shake my head.
It feels like cheating.

"*Ring* it,"
he says again,
and shakes it
just a little

so it jangles.

I hear Mom's voice in my head—
first is what it's for.

The bell hangs
inches from my face,
the bright noon sunlight
setting the copper
on fire.

My fingers itch to take it.
I want to take it.
But . . . it wasn't a perfect swim.
I wasn't perfect.

Next to me,
Dad can't stand it any longer.
He hugs me tight
like he is afraid to let me go again.
His heart is a hummingbird,
mine a creaky clock.
His flannel shirt is soaked.
I don't know where his rain jacket went—
probably lost to the lake.

He takes the bell from Arch
and hands it to me.

"Here's an experiment," he suggests,

like we are testing bubbles on the deck.
"See if it sounds different
when you ring it
not because you *earned* it
but just . . . because."

It's an offer,
not an order.
He waits.

I hold the bell,
feel the weight of it,
which is hardly anything at all.

I've thought about this moment for months.
All the hours of training
snuck in when adults weren't watching
and all the hours in the library
researching weather patterns and timetables
and all the nights spent awake
envisioning every mile
so I would be ready.

There is no video to prove what I did.
But today I managed something
that no one my age ever has—
     I swam twelve miles
     in six hours.

At twelve years old,

I am a marathoner.

Mom always says
perfection isn't possible
without sacrifice.
Maybe she's right.

I look at Dad and Arch,
who saved me.

Maybe perfection *isn't* possible
without sacrifice.
But I don't want
to be perfect
if it means
ending up
alone.

I shake the bell
with all my might.
It *does* sound different,
    a bluebird whistling on a fence
    instead of a rooster's caw.

The seagulls throw a hissy fit.
Dad lets out the most ridiculous hoot.
Arch whistles loud and off-key and races down the shore.

I watch it all
a little outside myself

like a cloud overhead.

When he comes back from the water,
Arch places an absolutely disgusting
ring of tangled weeds on my head
like a crown.
It smells like rotting bread—
slightly sweet,
not as terrible
as it could be.

I smile up at him.
Everything hurts.

There are so many bigger things
than this swim.
Mom is still not here,
and I don't know if she's coming back
or if I want her to.

I watch two sandpipers fight over a Twix wrapper
while the sun warms my shoulders
and the sand sticks to my wrinkled feet,
then I wipe away tears
I didn't know I'd cried
with the corner of my towel.

Maybe what they say about avalanches
is true about life too.
You have to cry to find out

which way is
up.

I hug my towel closer
and then stand
to let Dad and Arch lead me
on wobbly legs to the car
so we can go to IHOP,
eat a million pancakes,
and plan my next swim.

ACKNOWLEDGMENTS

Reka Simonsen gets
major credits
for the edits.

Keely Boeving started
as agent and became lifelong friend
in the end.

Alisha Monnin made
this cover a thing of beauty
for all to see.

Karyn Lee designed
a jacket for this book
that'll make every reader take a second look.

Jeannie Ng and Kaitlyn San Miguel copyedited
this wonky long poem
so well I want to hug them.

Chris Baron encouraged
my take
on poems with shape.

Lisa Fipps is an excellent writer
but an even "excellent-er" friend.
The end.

Kathleen Allen read
with empathy
and added authenticity.

Jody inspired
the bubble test,
and if I'm honest, all the rest.

My kiddos kept
me on my toes
by helping me rhyme aloud like pros.

The people of Lake Tahoe wooed
my heart to the West Coast
with that artsy vibe I love most.

The teachers and librarians doing
everything you can
to get books into kids' hands.